BLOOD ON THE BALL

Blood on the Ball

DIANA LEE

Contents

VI ~

This book is dedicated to the Duke City Chile Dogs. We never found any dismembered body parts, but there were many Saturday morning practices playing with the dogs in the summer sun.

Chapter 1

The Pound

It all started at the Valencia County Animal Shelter. Sylvia was there, walking up and down the rows, looking at the faces. This was the fault of her sister, Sonia, who had a talent for talking Sylvia into things she probably shouldn't do. You had to have someone in your life who would lead you astray from the easy path. It gave life its sparkle. Sonia was reading the kennel card.

"He doesn't even have a name. Seven months old. Owner surrender."

"Seven months? He's just a puppy! Who dumps a puppy at the pound?"

Sonia shook her head in agreement and continued scanning the kennel card. Sylvia looked into the kennel.

Mismatched eyes, one blue, one greenish amber, looked up at Sylvia through the kennel bars. The puppy was a mass of different colored speckles, with black and grey on his body transitioning to gold on his paws and face. The tail was beating back and forth, hopefully. Sylvia crouched down, poking her fingers through the bars for the puppy to chew on. The puppy offered an ear to scritch, which she did. He then turned to press his whole side against the kennel bars. Sylvia

1

scratched and petted him through the bars, while the puppy wiggled blissfully.

"Australian Cattle Dog. Male. Not fixed. No tricks listed. Doesn't say if he's potty trained."

"Oh, look at his tail! He has a raccoon tail!" Sonia looked through the kennel bars to confirm the ringed tail.

"Awww, how cute," she said and paused a moment, watching Sylvia's face as she interacted with the puppy. None of the cacophonic barking of the rest of the shelter mattered. The smells and stress faded away.

"All those little freckles all over. He's so cute. . . " Sylvia continued, not even noticing her sister had already pulled out the kennel card and went to find the shelter worker.

A few minutes later, a young man in an animal shelter polo walked up, smiling knowingly at Sonia as they both watched Sylvia tickle the ecstatic puppy through the cage bars. Finally, he spoke up. "Hi, I'm Tommy. He is a cutie. You want to meet the little monster?" Tommy unwrapped the leash he had looped around his neck and moved to open the kennel door.

Sylvia looked up and nodded. "Thanks," she remembered to say. She stood up and moved back, allowing the kennel worker to enter the cage and leash up the dog. As he did, the man stepped on a squeaker from one of the many destuffed and destroyed toys scattered around the cage.

As they let the puppy drag them around the little meet and greet area, Tommy gently probed about why Sylvia wanted a dog, what activities she would do with it, what she envisioned her day-to-day life with the dog would be like, whether she was familiar with cattle dogs, etc.

Sylvia nodded at her sister, who had retreated to a discrete distance to let her interact with the Animal Control guy and the puppy. "She's the one who inspired me to come look for a dog. I transferred here from work, but I have no family here and don't know anyone. My sister came up to visit for my birthday, and we started talking about how I am coming home to an empty house and doing too much screen time and not enough real time."

Tommy nodded encouragingly, "It can get a bit lonely when you move away from your family."

Actually, not so much, Sylvia thought. She did not voice it, though. Some things were better left unsaid. She did miss Sonia, though. And she tried hard to preserve that scrap of connection. Somehow, despite their upbringing, Sonia had managed to become a caring and empathetic person. Sylvia did her best to imitate her older sister. She tried to take the good bits from people around her in a scavenger hunt to somehow smoosh them into a whole person.

The animal control guy was staring at her, waiting for a response.

"Yeah, so I thought a dog, that would make me go out and walk it, and take it to classes and stuff. Might help me get out there a bit more."

Tommy chuckled. "Yeah, I suspect this little guy will keep you pretty busy. Cattle dogs can be pretty demanding in their need for exercise and training."

"That's exactly what I need right now. I want a demanding dog who will pull me out of myself."

"Okay, okay, I believe you! Just remember you were warned!" He said with a grin, holding up his hands in pretend defense, and then they headed back to do the paperwork.

On the way home from the pound, the two sisters stopped by the pet store and Sonia had fun throwing a ridiculous quantity of toys, treats, cards from trainers, and any other doggy paraphernalia that caught their eyes into the cart with the puppy, who desqueaked five toys before they even made it to the register. Sonia was trying to talk Sylvia into naming him Racoon, or Coon, for the tail. The cashier was laughing at them as they both fought to be the first to put their debit cards through the reader. By the time Sonia headed back home, the puppy was named Cyrus, and Sylvia realized she had a toothy, barky, little terror of a dog.

Two months later, Sylvia was sitting on the couch, talking on the phone with her sister, giving what had become the regular weekly update of things Cyrus had destroyed.

"Your kindle? He ate your kindle? Oh no, bad puppy!" said Sonia.

Sylvia looked down at the dog sprawled upside down across her lap, spotty feet up in the air, looking up at her with a toothy grin. "He's really sorry," she said. Sylvia playfully tried to grab the dog's lolling tongue while he pretended to try to bite her fingers. "Besides, it still works. There are just some tooth holes."

"Hmmmm..." said her sister.

"We're going to try some flyball."

"?"

"I dunno. Somebody in one of our obedience classes gave me info for some lady and I sent her an email. She said they have a tournament this weekend and so I am going to volunteer and see what it's about." Sylvia was now gently poking the various polka dots on Cyrus' belly while he swung his head back and forth, trying to bite her fingers, the raccoon tail thumping the couch and her leg.

"You are going to run in a tournament?"

"Nah, just volunteer, to check it out. I was looking at some videos Donna, the flyball lady, sent me and he jumped on the keyboard and nearly broke my computer! Do you wanna do some flyball, Cyrus? Huh? Wanna flyball?"

Cyrus whipped to his feet, stood on the arm of the chair and started barking in her ear. He had a particularly high-pitched, earsplitting bark.

"Are you sure you want something that makes him more excited?"

"Tennis balls, jumps, barking, I bet he'll love it!"

"hmmmmm..."

Chapter 2

Doggy Nascar

Sylvia fumbled attempting to pull the lever, while trying to read the cheat sheet written on an index card that was taped on the top of the flyball box. The barking echoed off the concrete floor, the painted cinderblock walls, and metal ceiling of the large fairgrounds building. "Second large hole from the left," she muttered to herself, then realized she didn't know if that was her left, or left looking at her? As she tried to stuff a tennis ball in the correct hole while holding back the activator lever, the other three balls she was trying to hold in her hands popped out and rolled away.

"Ahhhh sorry! Wait! Oh crap!"

She was chasing after the errant tennis balls off the rubber matting, but one had rolled out under the cross-hatched knee-high lattice and towards the crowd. "Ooops!"

"Where'd it go?"

"Here!"

It was a kid, maybe eight, with curly brown hair, holding the ball out towards her. His gaze was fixed to the left, though. Turning her head to see what he was looking at she saw a border whippet racing down the lane straight at her. With a panicked squeal, Sylvia jumped back in the well of the box, crammed a ball in whatever hole her hand found and braced for impact. The dog pulled up at the last minute twisted sideways, and hit the box with all four feet, triggering the spring-loaded mechanism to launch the tennis ball. Unfortunately, the dog's head was facing left, when Sylvia had loaded right. The ball bounced off the dog's brindle-striped haunch. The border whippet shot her a snipy look, ignored the ball, and raced back down the lane. A terrier-shaped blur appeared from the other lane, stole the abandoned tennis ball and raced down this lane after the border whippet. Whistles blew.

Sylvia watched as the handlers in team shirts grabbed the dogs, which were quickly sorted out and pulled over into their appropriate lanes. The handler in her lane, a tall, very fit young man with long, dark blonde hair pulled in a low ponytail, shouted something unintelligible at the other members of the team. He then kneeled on the rubber matting that defined the lane, pulling the border whippet so that the dog's back legs braced against his thighs like runner's feet on starting blocks. Ponytail man held the dog with his hands just over the dog's hips. The dog's head whipped around to stare at Sylvia with a laser focus. Everything got quiet. Everyone was waiting, staring at her. The judge was standing in the middle of the lanes between the flyball teams, wearing a black and white striped shirt. He stood, his hand raised to cue, whistle in his mouth ready to sound. Everything stopped. Every eye seemed fixed on her. Even the judge turned to look at her over his shoulder.

"The ball!" Someone yelled.

Startled, she shook off her daze, and Sylvia quickly stepped over to the bucket an older, gray-haired man was holding up towards her over the sideline fencing. The bucket, one of those plastic ones you get at home improvement stores, was painted in bright colors with paw prints. It was full of tennis balls with the team name stamped on them. Steve, that was the name of the grinning guy holding the bucket.

"It's okay, take your time. Don't get frazzled," he said.

"I'm sorry," she said as she fished around for tennis balls in the bucket.

"You're doing fine. Don't forget the little one for Fiest."

Sylvia squeezed a miniature tennis ball from the small fabric pocket attached to the side of the bucket.

"Get extras. Stuff them in the pockets of your apron. You are doing fine."

She tucked several extra tennis balls in the handsewn apron she was wearing. Donna had pushed it into her hands just before Sylvia had stepped into the ring to start box loading. There were little cartoon dogs and tennis balls all over it. The apron was ridiculous and adorable.

"You ready?" asked Steve. "Take a breath. Read the cheat sheet. Remember, Stealth, Slick, and Venom all load right. Fiest is last. He does the little ball on the left."

Sylvia nodded, murmuring the list of dog names to herself, and stepped back into the well of the flyball box. She carefully pulled the lever on the top of the box until it clicked, and then loaded the tennis ball on the right. Leaning forward, she braced her knees against the box. You are a sandbag, she told herself. You are a tennis-ball loading sandbag weight to stop the wooden flyball box from flipping up when the dogs hit it to trigger the release of the ball. She looked up, met the judge's eyes and nodded. You've got this, she told herself. The judge grinned, gave her a thumbs up, and turned to face the teams. The whistle blew and the building erupted with handler's screams, dogs' barking and the chaos that was flyball.

Donna Perry, the lady she had emailed back and forth with prior to coming this tournament, had tried to warn her. With the apron had been a little care package, including earplugs and band aids. Even after watching the chaotic looking videos, Sylvia still had not realized what she was getting into. This was her first time actually seeing flyball and maybe volunteering to boxload was taking on too much. However, Sylvia had wanted to make a good impression and earn some brownie points. She really needed an outlet for Cyrus' puppy energy. The obedience club had given her the contact information for a lady who was the captain of a flyball team. When Sylvia contacted her, Donna had talked about jumps and tennis balls and, honestly, it had sounded like something a bonkers little cattle dog with a racoon striped tail could really get into. When Donna had mentioned that they were a little short on team members, Sylvia had jumped on the chance to really dig in and see what this flyball was all about.

She must have managed to get through the other three heats of the race, because she looked up from trying to load another tennis ball to see everyone was gathering their things and leaving the ring. A man was standing there, holding another flyball box. She needed to move hers. She reached for the hand holds on either side and braced herself to lift it.

"Wait, let me get that for you!" Steve had reappeared and quickly lifted the box out of the way. He carried it off to join the collection of similar contraptions to the side of the ring.

"Thanks!" said Sylvia, as she quickly gathered what stray tennis balls she could see and stepped out of the way. People wearing "Paws Afire" shirts quickly replaced the box with a similar one made of fiberglass, with their team logo printed on the top. They set up a contraption of plastic gutter pieces in front of it and dogs started bouncing off the box. There were suddenly so many people and dogs in the very small box loading area. Sylvia stepped over the short fence out of the ring and joined Steve on the sidelines where he was standing by their team's box and ball bucket.

"They are trying to get some practice in before they start," he explained.

Sylvia watched the elaborate dance of loading a tennis ball, placing a section of plastic gutter in front of the box, releasing the dog, moving the gutter, dog hitting the box, and then immediately pulling that dog off to the side to let another dog go. There seemed to be sleek, over-excited dogs bark-screaming everywhere.

"It's very well-choreographed," she observed. Each dog seemed to have its own plastic gutter arrangement, uniquely customized with duct tape, pool noodles, and multiple sections attached together. Specific people seemed to be in charge of each dog's gutter prop. Steve explained that the teams were only allowed a very short practice time in the ring before they needed to run their heats. Soon, her own puppy, Cyrus, would be doing that. Sylvia and this big bear of a grey-haired man walked back to join the rest of the team, who were sitting in an arc of various folding camp chairs eating pizza. It looked like really good pizza, all kinds of savory toppings. Sylvia tried to remember their names from the brief introductions, earlier that morning. She wasn't sure if it helped or hurt that about half the team was named some version of "Jennifer."

Donna was the older woman with straight, greyish-brown hair cut shoulder length, and bangs. She was the captain of the team. Dan, her husband was tall and lanky, covering up thinning hair with a baseball cap with an Isotopes logo. Sitting next to Dan was Jen. She had the little Jack Russels, Fiest and Fiend. Jen had long, dark, thick hair and decisive manner. There were two other members of the team, a woman named Jennifer and the good-looking blonde guy. Sylvia and Steve had dodged around them as the other two argued intensely before looking up, catching a glance at her and stalking off together out the side door. Steve had just given a shrug in response to Sylvia's questioning glance.

Sylvia tried to shake off the unpleasant interaction. What could be their problem with her? She hadn't even met either of them before! The blond guy seemed pretty intense, so maybe he was just frustrated with her ineptness at box loading? Everyone else seemed so nice and welcoming.

"So, what did you think?" asked Dan, grinning in anticipation. Sylvia mentally switched gears to try to let go of whatever the issue was with those two.

"Wow! A lot happening, all at once! I am sorry I couldn't keep up."

"You did fine," assured Donna, glancing up from a notebook she had been writing notes in.

"Flyball is crazy. You'll get the hang of it before you know it," Jen told her, while offering her a paper plate with pizza.

"It's been described as the 'NASCAR of Dog Sports.'" Said Don.

"I could see that," laughed Sylvia.

Don went on to explain about the history of flyball. There was something about David Letterman, and it was probably really interesting, but Sylvia couldn't hear most of what he said. She smiled and nodded at what seemed like appropriate times until his wife distracted him with something about the seed times and the notes in her notebook.

Sylvia went over to one of the crates and released her puppy. Somehow, she got a leash on the mass of black, white and gold ticking and wiggle, and carried him out the side door to visit the grass. She wandered the fairgrounds outside the building where they were running flyball, trying to find a place a little less overstimulating for little Cyrus. He was barking at every dog he saw. There were LOTS of dogs, everywhere.

"You're going to have your hands full with that one. Baby cattlemonster isn't he?" asked an older, grandmotherly lady, passing by. The lady was holding the leash to a beautiful Golden Retriever.

"Yeah," said Sylvia, with a smile to the adolescent puppy in her arms. Cyrus spotted something and was frantically trying writhe his way free. It was like trying to hold onto a seal on meth. Then the barking began. With a quick apology, Sylvia headed off the opposite direction of whatever it was that Cyrus was after.

"Give 'em hell!" the lady stage whispered at Cyrus, before moving on with a friendly wave at Sylvia. She had delicately coifed snowy hair and an elegantly dignified manner. The back of her shirt read "we LOVE balls, with a heart-shaped tennis ball. Her golden paced beside her, tail waiving in serene contentment.

Sylvia continued wandering the grounds until she found a spot in between some rows of bushes that seemed to cut off the view of Things to be Barked At. She set Cyrus down in the grass. The puppy started sniffing and circling, but kept stopping to stare suspiciously at random noises. "Hurry up, Cyrus. Go potty." Cyrus barked at a leaf. Sylvia resigned herself to a bit of a wait. Turning her head, she caught sight of Jen, standing a few feet away holding the leashes of her two terriers as they did the potty dance.

"Oh, I'm sorry, I didn't see you, there."

"Don't apologize. I just realized they needed out, too, and thought I would walk with you."

"I was a little distracted," Sylvia confessed.

"Stop apologizing," laughed Jen. "You're fine. You are doing fine. Your puppy is being a fine puppy."

"Okay, sor – Okay, and NOT sorry."

"That's right, you're FINE!"

"FINE!" Sylvia was chuckling. Jen grinned at her. Sylvia noticed that the voices she was hearing in the background suddenly got louder, and they didn't sound fine. Cyrus' head shot up and his ears perked in the direction of the voices. Jen rolled her eyes and turned her head toward the sound.

"Wow, Jennifer's really giving it to him," she observed.

Sylvia looked at Jen in confusion. The other woman nodded at a gap in the bushes. Sylvia sidled over and peered through the gap. Two people were arguing. The good-looking blonde guy, Jonathan, was faced off against Jennifer, the other woman on the flyball team. Hands were waiving in quick, emphatic gestures. Sylvia was finding her initial response to Jonathon of "Wow, he's pretty!" really wearing off.

"Jeesh, they are really going at it. What's wrong. Are they always like this?" asked Sylvia, after stepping closer to Jen and lowering her voice. She wondered if pretty boy and Karen-haired Jennifer were a thing. Maybe they were one of those couples, all drama.

Jen shook her head, then nodded pointedly at Cyrus. Sylvia looked a question.

"Cyrus? What has he done?" Hearing his name, the puppy abandoned his sniffing and sat looking up at her, wagging his tail. Sylvia was surprised at how defensive she felt towards the puppy she had for such a short time. In her defense, he was a lot, for such a little puppy. It amazed her how enthralled to those mismatched eyes she was. Sylvia fumbled in her treat pouch to reward him for paying attention to his name. Jen made a shushing gesture. She ushered Sylvia further away. She then explained that Jennifer had taken one look at Cyrus, and recognized him for the puppy her rescue had just placed with Jonathan. That certainly explained the intense whispered questioning Jennifer had subjected Donna and the rest of the team to when she spotted Sylvia walking into the building with her puppy this morning.

"Jennifer is ripping Jonathan a new one because he dumped that puppy at a shelter as soon as Donna accepted him on the team. He used that puppy to get in good with her, then got rid of him," Jen explained. This sounded complicated. All Sylvia wanted was to have fun with her dog, not to be caught up in drama.

"I don't want to cause problems..." Sylvia started.

Jen shook her head. "Jonathan is the problem. And he deserves what he is getting. He used Jennifer's rescue and he abandoned that poor puppy."

"Maybe it's not the same…"

"He admitted it! Besides, one green eye, one blue. One white paw and three black paws. The pattern of rings on his tail. The shape and intensity of his ticking." Jen lifted a finger for each point. Sylvia looked at her little polka dotted, ring-tailed puppy, rolling happily in the leaves and grass. She had loved the unique look of him in the shelter, all black and white and gold speckles, with a ringed tail like a raccoon.

The other woman continued, "That's the same puppy. And Jonathan is an asshat. You will realize that soon after interacting with him."

Maybe the women had been overheard, maybe not, but the argument in the background had gone silent. Jennifer and Jonathan had disappeared from view. Maybe they had just moved out of earshot.

Sylvia wasn't sure about jumping in a group with all this drama, but everyone else seemed nice. As she attended practices in the weeks following, she learned to just avoid Jonathan. Jennifer, however, quickly became a constant source of help and encouragement. Newlyweds Jenny and her husband, Luis, joined the team with their sweet ditzy Australian Shepherd, Flicker, about the same time as Sylvia. They provided a lighthearted counterpoint to the tensions between Jennifer and Jonathan.

Chapter 3

The Foot

"Don't worry, Cyrus, you'll get to run with the real team," Sylvia assured her cattle dog as she drove. "We won't let that Jonathan and his stinky border whippets keep you down." Cyrus seemed oblivious to her concern. His mismatched eyes, one blue, one green, were fixed on the scenery passing by in the bright summer sunshine out the windows. They were on the way to meet the team for their regular Saturday morning flyball practice. Lente Lane, the road they were driving on, passed by large houses on big lots with multicar garages and horse pastures. Sylvia wasn't sure if this would be considered bougie hobby farm or bougie suburban.

It all made her little very non-bougie Honda seem out of place. All the houses had large lots. Some of the lots were pastures with farm animals, some had rodeo equipment, there was a vineyard, and some were just large, mown fields. She made the final turn to Cinder Lane, where it intersected with the street she was driving on in a T. On one side of the corner, a grey Arabian paced the fence line, prancing and arching his neck, flicking his tail, and tossing his head. Sylvia loved admiring the faint dapple pattern in his coat that glimmered in the sun, and the streaks of lighter and darker hair in his mane and tail. Two buckskin mares in the pasture on the other side of the street from the Arabian seemed to share Sylvia's appreciation.

Cyrus' excited whining transformed into a howl as they turned down Cinder Lane. He was a dog that focused on essentials, and the street that led to flyball practice was rapidly becoming quite recognizable to him. She laughingly encouraged the dog by imitating him. The blue Honda pulled up to the metal gate in the gravel at the driveway at Steve's house, windows rolled down, both occupants howling like coyotes.

She walked up to the gate and was greeted by several wiggling Australian Shepherds and Border Collies. Jenny came over holding a tennis ball launcher. Today, her hair was a mass of beaded black braids that clicked against each other as she moved. Last week it was some sort of airy lime green confection. Jenny and Luis seemed equally infatuated with each other and it made Sylvia smile each time she saw them. Sylvia suspected that Jenny's ever-changing hair was actually a series of wigs, but the young woman was new to the team and she didn't know her well enough to ask directly. Jenny waved at Sylvia and then lured the various dogs back to the open pasture in the back of the house. Sylvia opened the gate, drove through, and parked the little Honda in front of the barn, under the shade of the tall cottonwood trees. She quickly pulled the gate closed again, making sure to latch the lever and drop the stopper pole in its hole. No dogs were getting that open. Then she reached out to the handle of the passenger door of her car.

As soon as his owner opened the door, Cyrus burst out of the car, wound his way in a speckled streak through the shady trees of Steve's back yard, and slipped under the back fence to join the pack. "Incoming!" Sylvia yelled in warning to the four women out in the field. The barking dogs were chasing tennis balls thrown by Jenny. Jen, Jennifer, and Donna stood in a group in the sunny field, watching the dogs chase the ball and each other. Sylvia could hear the older women's voices egging the dogs to "Get that cattle dog! Don't let him steal the ball EVERY time!" It sounded like Cyrus was taking over the game, as usual. Please don't be too much of a turd, Sylvia thought at her dog, then she turned and walked through the open doorway of the barn.

Steve was loading wooden jumps and flyball boxes in a small cart. Dan was standing next to Steve, handing him pieces of wooden flyball equipment brightly painted in the team's colors of blue, purple and white. Dan was Donna's husband. He and Luis, Jenny's tall and graceful young husband, were gathered around a small garden tractor with a trailer attached. They were pretending to help Steve load and talking smack about some politician. Sylvia followed the cart as Steve drove the tractor to tow the trailer out to the practice field. Brightly painted wooden jump pieces began dropping off the cart. She picked up the jumps that fell off and carried them out to the practice field.

It was a lovely summer morning, full of sunshine and the sound of barking dogs. Most of the dogs were in a swirling barking mass, the sun gleaming off their fur like the scales of a shoal of fish. That swirling mass would suddenly reform to an arrow and sprint off after the tennis balls as they launched. Two dogs broke off to go bark at the fence. Sylvia and Donna walked over. The dogs were barking at a couple of massive shepherd mixes on the other side of the fence. The women tried to break it up, with the rest of the people coming over to help redirect the dogs.

"Careful, they don't break through the fence," Steve cautioned, his voice tight with tension.

"They were the dogs that got your sheep?" asked Jen.

"Yes," Steve confirmed.

"You're sure?"

"Yes. Saw it. Couldn't do anything. They are vicious."

There was a collective wince. Everyone focused on getting the flyball dogs away from the wire fence.

"Go on! Get out of here!" Steve sternly told the neighbor dogs. They froze staring him straight in the eyes. "Shoo! Go home!" After a few moments, the neighbor dogs nonchalantly turned and melted back into the overgrown brush.

As Sylvia helped stuff dogs in crates, she heard Luis ask where Jonathan was. All he got in response was a generalized shrug from Donna and "I guess we will have to practice without him. Again."

Jonathan was the Hot Shot Handler. He had a pack of border whippets, slick otters of dogs, that were quick as thought. Sylvia had heard through team gossip that he had appeared with them several months ago and quickly took over all the spots on the "A" team except for the height dog, which was always one of Jen's Jack Russell Terriers. Jonathan and his ringer dogs came from a team in Texas whose dogs were famous for setting and breaking the records. He had come to this little Podunk flyball team in this little Podunk town to be a big fish in a little pond. Or, perhaps the rumors were true that he had been blackballed in Texas because of his prima donna attitude. Jonathan's dogs filled most of the spaces on the racing team. Jonathan ran start. He had other team members run his other dogs rather than their own dogs, because his dogs were so much faster. Donna and Jonathan clashed on who was actually in charge. They had a big one last week, and Jonathan tended to blow off practice when he didn't get his way.

"Cyrus is ready to do a few runbacks. Sylvia needs to practice handling a dog, just in case Jonathan doesn't make it to the tournament," Donna continued. Sylvia nodded in acknowledgement and went to dig Cyrus' favorite tug out of her backpack. As she fumbled around, looking for the quacking duck, she heard Dan and Jennifer talking to Steve about calling animal control on his neighbor. Dan was really pushing it, but Steve hunched his shoulders. If Steve called animal control and told them the neighbor's dogs killed his sheep, the dogs would be put down. Being over six feet tall, with bristling grey hair and beard didn't stop Steve from looking like a reluctant kid. Steve was too much of a softie to confront his neighbor.

"Sylvia, get your dog! Let's get started!" Donna sounded a little impatient.

She opened the crate, but no dog came out. Sylvia looked at his crate, but it was empty. Cyrus wasn't in it. She realized that he must have eluded the general doggie round up. Sneaky little turd. She glanced around and spied the speckled cattle dog on the far side of the field, lying near the neighbor's fence line, chewing on something.

"Troublemaker," she muttered, then called out "Cyrus! Come here!"

Cyrus gave a guilty flinch, then picked up his prize and trotted even further away. Sylvia sighed and rolled her eyes.

"Puppy Turd," she said, then started trudging toward her cattle dog and his treasure.

"What did you find, you heathen?" Sylvia asked him, as she approached. Considering they practiced in this field every Saturday morning, she would have assumed all the potential treasures would have been claimed long ago. Plus, Steve's dogs had run of the field every day. Alas, he had obviously found something precious.

A couple of her teammates snickered, used to Cyrus finding his own entertainment. They continued setting up the jumps and flyball boxes to form the two practice lanes, leaving Sylvia to sort out her naughty dog. "How far apart are the jumps?" asked Luis. He was holding several painted wood jump uprights and the wooden crossbars.

"Ten feet," answered Dan, Donna, and Steve, in unison. Steve placed the flyball box, a heavy, wooden contraption, and tested the spring loading mechanism. Luis and Jenny began pacing out from the box, fifteen feet, set up a jump, ten more feet, next jump, ten more feet, another jump, until there were two rows of parallel jumps, four jumps in each row, leading up to the flyball boxes. A person called a box loader would stand on the knee well of the boxes to brace them so the boxes wouldn't tip or move when the dogs hit them. Donna brought the buckets of the tennis balls over near the flyball boxes. Steve and Don loaded tennis balls and set the trigger mechanism. Then everyone watched Sylvia follow her dog on a slow, frustrating, chase inside the parameter of the fence line. Every time she got close, he would grab whatever it was and trot a little further off. She caught up to him under the trees at the far end of the field. Leaning close, she grabbed his collar, then looked at what he was dragging around.

"Oh, GOD, CYRUS, WHAT DO YOU HAVE?!"

The unmistakable fear in her shout stopped the snickers and brought everyone running. They all stood in a circle, staring down at the speckled dog' precious chew toy.

It was an expensive-looking blueish green sneaker with purple laces. Unfortunately for whomever it originally belonged to, a foot was still in it.

Chapter 4

Aren't We Going to Report It?

"What did the police tell Steve about ... it?" Jenny asked. She was walking her black tri-colored Australian Shepherd, Flicker, down the path that bordered Mariposa Park. Her wig today was a cloud of corkscrew curls that bounced with each step, in time with the bobbing of her dog's perfectly triangular ear tips. Flicker was outfitted in an ergohund harness in her signature color of purple, and the matching leash had delicate little birds printed on it. Jenny was also dressed in a purple teeshirt and shorts, with perfectly matched purple hiking shoes, a purple treat bag attached to her waist, with a purple bird-shaped poopbag dispenser full of purple bags dangling from it. Donna's black and white border collies, Guiness and Porter, slunk steadily forward on their more utilitarian leashes, white tail tips waiving. Cyrus' leash was braided fleece in the team colors. He weaved back and forth, peeing on sagebrush and cacti, and randomly jolting Sylvia's arm.

"Nothing," Donna finally answered Jenny's question.

There was a pause. When it became obvious that no other details were forthcoming, "I guess they aren't going to keep us updated. It's an active investigation or..." Sylvia speculated.

"No, he hasn't reported it," Donna clarified. The other two women stopped and stared at Donna.

Sensing an opportunity in the distraction, Cyrus attempted to pee on Guiness' head as she sniffed a bush. Fortunately, Sylvia gave a quick, two-handed tug on the leash to prevent it, though it nearly knocked the dog over. He gave his owner a betrayed look and darted under the three leashes of the other dogs to create a quick tangle. Once everyone was untangled, the conversation continued.

"Steve hasn't reported it? Why?" asked Jenny.

"He, I don't know, Jennifer and him think it's from that homeless guy who camps in the woods behind the crazy neighbor's place," Donna answered.

Jenny and Sylvia exchanged a look. Cyrus took the moment to lock his gaze in on an approaching dog. His entire speckled body tensed and he started barking. Sylvia swore over her lapse in attention as the group in a unanimous, unspoken decision reversed direction. She worked on drawing his attention with nose touches for treats. When she got Cyrus behaving (after his fashion) again, she continued the previous conversation:

"Even if it was the homeless guy, we still need to report it. The police have to find where the rest of him is and recover him and notify the family, if he has one, and bury him, and stuff."

"I hope it's not the homeless guy," said Jenny.

Sylvia nodded.

Donna said, "Steve is worried that it will get Cyrus in trouble, or cause trouble with the crazy neighbor."

"Why would Cyrus get in trouble?" Sylvia's tone was defensive, but more bewildered.

"Because he was eating a dead guy," Donna pointed out.

"The guy was already dead!"

There was a pause, while Sylvia realized she may be being a bit callus.

"I don't know. Jennifer has Steve all freaked out that it will just cause trouble."

"He HAS to report it. If he is too worried to do it, then I will," Sylvia stated. "He will get in trouble if he doesn't. Plus, that guy's family needs to know, the dead guy's family, I mean."

"Do you really think someone is dead?" Jenny's usually cheerful voice sounded rather lost. Flicker looked up at her, questioningly.

"Living people don't usually lose their feet, Jenny," Donna spoke more sharply than she intended. She glanced at the young woman in apology, then continued, "We'll talk to him."

The three women and their dogs continued on their walk around the park. Eventually, they followed the path down to the fenced baseball fields and wound their way in through an open gate. The dogs were let off leash to run in random circles and bark at each other, while the women continued talking.

"I still haven't heard from Jonathan. I think you are going to have to be prepared to run Cyrus." Sylvia nodded in acknowledgement. Donna was the team captain. It was her call, if she wanted to replace Jonathan. Besides, Cyrus had been training with the team for several months. In practice, he alternated between awesome and awful.

They watched as the speckled cattle dog sprinted after the border collies and Aussie, easily overtaking the other dogs, and then spun around to head them off. His feet tangled and Cyrus ended up rolling like a bowling ball. Being a cattle dog, and thus made of rubber, he bounced back and immediately took off after the others again.

"Jonathan will probably still show up. He sulks for a bit, but then he comes back."

"He will be there for the tournament. He never misses them."

"Jonathan pushed it too far this time. The tournament is almost here. We're running out of time. I am sick of this crap. Steve agrees. So does everyone else. Sylvia is at every practice. Cyrus is fast, even if he is a bit of an idiot," Donna paused for another quick apology glance at Cyrus' owner, who just chuckled and nodded in agreement at the assessment of her dog. Cyrus was smart, but that didn't preclude him acting like an idiot. "Jennifer was right about that dog. He has a lot of potential, even if hot shot Jonathan couldn't see it. I'm the captain. It's my decision. Cyrus is going to run," Donna said.

Jenny flashed Sylvia a triumphant smile behind Donna's back.

"So, he had better stop eating people." Sylvia winced, but Donna didn't apologize for that one. Honestly, though, it seemed a reasonable requirement.

"God, I hope so," said Sylvia.

After the dogs were all panting and seeking shade, the women leashed them up and walked the path back around the park. It took all three of them, but they did manage to keep Cyrus out of the duck pond this time. Safely loaded in the car, Sylvia took a moment to relish the victory. Cyrus was going to run in a tournament. All the work, all the training, the obedience classes, the counter-conditioning to control his heel-nipping drive, it all was going to pay off!

Jonathan was supposed to be Cyrus' owner. Several months ago, when Jennifer had the adolescent cattle dog puppy come through her rescue, Paws and Reload, Jennifer had the rescue place him with Jonathan as an experienced sport home that would be able to channel that drive. Jonathan expressed enthusiasm for the idea just long enough to get in with the little flyball team, then had dumped the puppy at a shelter, almost immediately. Sylvia had found the polka dotted bundle of puppy teeth and attitude at the shelter and fallen in love. She brought the puppy home and waded through the world of cattle monster attitude. Jennifer had found out that Jonathan had dumped the dog when Sylvia showed up with Cyrus as a new flyball recruit. To say Jennifer was not a fan of Jonathan after that was an understatement.

So, the possibility that Jonathan's reject dog would be taking his prized border whippet's place on the team, even for one tournament, was particularly karmic. Sylvia knew that Jonathan would probably deign to show up for practice again and worm his way back in to the team's good graces. But, that was then, and this is now. "I think we need a puppy burger," Sylvia told Cyrus and turned off at the McDonalds drive through. The voice over the intercom when she was placing the order seemed particularly skilled at sifting Sylvia's voice through Cyrus' excited barking. She wondered if she was getting known as the crazy dog lady at that particular McDonalds.

Sylvia knew where Jenny stood on the matter of Jonathan, and Donna had said that everyone on the team supported her decision to boot Jonathan for the tournament. She was still surprised when she saw the group text from Donna about the change. There was a message from Jennifer asking if Cyrus was really running on the main team for the tournament. When Donna confirmed, Jennifer texted back "Good. Fuck Jonathan." It probably would have been more diplomatic to not do that on the group text where he was included. Apparently, there was really no love lost between those two. There was no response from Jonathan on the group text, but Sylvia thought he probably would work on Donna and Steve privately to get them to change their minds.

Lying in bed that night, Cyrus curled in a ball at her feet, Sylvia's mind kept circling back to finding Cyrus, chewing on the shoe, and realizing there was still a foot. She couldn't stop thinking of that shoe. It was a Salomon, a high-end running shoe. Blueish green under the dirt and blood and ,,, other stuff. With vivid purple laces. It was definitely a little to "hot shot" for what you would think a homeless person living in the woods would be wearing.

Chapter 5

The Hand

Another sunny Saturday morning, and as Sylvia's ancient
Honda turned the corner past the dapple-grey Arabian
stallion flirting with the buckskin mares, Cyrus started howling in anticipation. Sylvia didn't join in today. She kept
thinking of that shoe. When she turned into Steve's driveway, she quickly parked her car and strode over to where
Steve was loading the cart.

"Hi Sylvia! Excited about Cyrus running in the tournament?"

She was too distracted to respond to Steve's good-natured
cheer.

"Donna said you haven't called the police?"

Steve paused. Sylvia marveled at how you could actually
see his shoulders tense up. Then he wordlessly just continued loading the cart. She felt like she was like scolding a
child.

"Steve, you HAVE to."

He looked at her with a pained expression. "Just drop it,
okay."

"But,"

"Hey guys!" It was Jen. Steve quickly redirected the conversation, asking Jen questions about random things and dragging the trailer out to the field. Jen and Sylvia followed him, Jen mouthing "What's going on?" at Sylvia. Sylvia just rolled her eyes. As they passed through the gate, Cyrus and Jen's Jack Russels sprinted to the far side of the field and began digging at the fence line.

"Please don't dig up any more feet," Syvia joked, then winced. Steve started throwing jumps down.

"Hey, what did the police say? Did they figure out who it was?" Jen's question hung in the air. It was amazing that his shoulders looked even tighter. He was like a kid in a '60's sitcom trying to avoid getting in trouble.

Sylvia and Steve's eyes met.

"You have GOT to report it, Steve!" said Sylvia.

"You haven't called the police, yet?" Steve avoided Jen's gaze like a naughty toddler, a burly toddler over six feet tall with a grizzled beard and grey hair. Jen set her hands on her hips and stepped in front of him to force him to look at her.

Steve was saved from responding because Cyrus and the two little terriers started squabbling. There was a flicker of fur along the other side of the fence. Jen and Sylvia ran over to break it up and redirect. Jen tucked her brown and white terriers, Fiest under one arm and Fiend under the other. Sylvia grabbed Cyrus' collar and drug him away from the fence line, shouting at the huge GSD mix to back off. Instead, it vaulted the fence. Sylvia scooped up Cyrus and the women fled toward the barn with their dogs. A shot rang out and the shepherd mix paused, giving them and Steve enough time to make it to the barn and slam the door shut.

The neighbor dog snarled and thumped against the door. Sylvia could hear the sound of scratching against the wood, trying to find a crack. There were low growls coming from Cyrus and the Jack Russells. The cattle dog wiggled free from her hold and rushed to the door, barking. Sylvia grabbed him and pulled him back.

"You just shush," Sylvia told her dog, "You're definitely not helping." He met her eyes with that creepy understanding intelligence that some dogs have, then stared at the door. He was quiet, but his body language seemed to communicate that the dog thought he could handle it, if they would just open the door and let him.

Jen was dialing her phone,

"Jenny, yeah, don't come in. Don't open the gate! Stay in your car!"

Sylvia quickly pulled out her phone to send a group text to everyone. She saw Steve fumbling with his gun.

"It's out of bullets," he said.

"At least you slowed him down so we could make it in here."

"Good thing you had it on you!"

"Yeah, I have been carrying it when I go out to the field after the incident with sheep."

"In your own yard?! Steve! You need to call the police about those dogs!"

And, you need to call them about the foot, thought Sylvia. Now wasn't the time, though to get into that.

In the background, Jen's voice was explaining the emergency to 911. Sylvia saw Steve's eyes widen in panic.

"NO! Don't call them!" Steve shouted. He tried to reach for the woman's phone.

Jen warded him off with a quelling look and continued the call, turning her shoulder to Steve.

"Do you need me to stay on the line? Are you sure?" She concluded the call and said, "They are sending animal control."

As they waited, listening to the hound from hell attempt to break down the door, Jen pushed Steve on why he hadn't reported the neighbor dogs being dangerous, and then morphed into asking why he hadn't reported the foot. He expressed concern that Cyrus would be put down. Steve said didn't want the dog killed because of the unfortunate death of a homeless man, and he didn't want the neighbor's vicious dogs put down because their owner was an idiot survivalist who wanted to breed the ultimate war dog. Jen and Sylvia just stared at him for a moment.

"Dude, you are too softhearted," said Jen. "And softheaded. They won't put Cyrus down because of his revolting chew toy. And those neighbor dogs are a menace."

"And, it wasn't a homeless man." Sylvia's voice was so quiet. She wasn't sure they even heard her. They apparently did hear though. They both were staring, so she had to continue. "It was a Salomon shoe. Blue Green. With purple laces."

"Homeless guy had nice shoes?"

Jen was not getting it. Steve wasn't helping. He just stood there looking guilty. Sylvia had to explain.

"No. Jonathan had nice shoes. Blue Salomons." Sylvia was trying to catch Steve's eyes, to figure out what was going on with him. The older man abruptly abandoned his attempt to avoid the discussion.

"With purple laces," confirmed Steve. His eyes met Sylvia's, then Jen's.

"Shit," said Jen.

While they were processing that bit of info, there was a disturbance in the pattern of barking and thumping on the door. Then the sound of tires and a blaring horn. Some shouting, shattered glass, a brief scream. A shotgun popped, a yelp, sudden silence and then footsteps and a voice shouting, "Is everyone okay in there?"

They looked at each other in the dim light of the shed.

"I think so?" Sylvia's answer was more a question than a response.

"Can you come out, now?"

"Ummm," said Jen, "will anything try to kill us?"

"It's okay, Jen. You can come out." At Donna's decisive re-assurance, Jen tentatively cracked the door open. The driveway was full of flashing lights and police cars. Luis was standing by his car, hugging a crying Jenny. Donna was sitting in her car, watching the doorway to the barn. Jennifer stood with several police officers over the body of giant German shepherd-ish dog, quietly talking with them.

"The dog came from over there," declared Jen, pointing. She watched the sea of heads turn to follow her gesture. The crowd of police and animal control walked through the trees to the gate, across the practice field over to the far fence line. The members of the flyball team trailed after. Jen and Sylvia pointed to the spot the dog had vaulted the fence.

"He jumped that?" asked one of the officers, and Jen and Sylvia nodded. The police man made a low whistle of admiration and went over to examine the spot in the fence more closely. Something caught his attention. He bent down, reaching through the fence to nudge some leaves and brush detritus aside.

"Hey, what's that?" he asked.

"Huh?" The other police officer looked up from where he was standing in front of Steve, flipping through a notebook looking for a blank page.

"Come look at this. Richie, I think you need to see this."

Richie, or Rick, or whatever his partner was calling him today, walked over and looked at what the other man was pointing at.

"Oh, fuck, is that a ..."

"Omyfuc...."

"Shut up and get the crime scene tape. Now."

The man shut up, turned on his heel, and sprinted back to the police cars in the driveway, the various items on his equipment belt jangling discordantly.

Very quietly and unobtrusively, Sylvia edged her way closer and peaked through the fence. It was a hand, lying under the bushes at the fence line, on the neighbor's side of the property. The thick, stubby, grayish fingers were curled around a handful of dead leaf litter. The were tooth holes puncturing it, partially obscuring a tattoo of what looked like the "don't tread on me" snake, but very little blood. The wrist end appeared gnawed. It looked like it had been there awhile, and all the blood was licked away by, she assumed, the neighbor's hellish dogs. Fortunately, Cyrus hadn't found this one. The other officer glanced up, saw her looking, and the members of the flyball team were quickly shooed away to stand in a nervous herd by the barn, holding their confused and frustrated dogs by leashes and collars.

Jen, practical person she was, looked around and realized they were going to be there for a bit. She pulled out a crate and stuffed her terriers in it. Sylvia and Jen made a brief assembly line of pulling crates out, setting them up and inserting dogs in them. Soon all the dogs were contained. Sylvia met Jen's eyes. She edged over to stand right by him and whispered in Steve's ear:

"Where's it at?"

Steve stared back at her, confused.

"The foot. Where did you put the foot?"

Luis was standing by the doorway of the barn, watching the police process the scene, but his head whipped around as he heard the whispers and he started making frantic shushing movements.

"Steve, where did you put it?" Jen persisted.

Comprehension dawned in Steve's eyes and his glance flicked toward the burn barrels tucked away behind the barn.

"You BURNED it?" Jen's voice was definitely more than a whisper. Luis was looking rather panicked; his attention divided between the preoccupied police and the rather incriminating conversation of his companions.

Steve shook his head and mouthed "Not yet." Jen and Sylvia both rolled their eyes and Sylvia pried Steve's handgun out of his hand. She discretely set it on a work table, behind a pile of tools. Luis' eyes widened. Sylvia roller her eyes at him, then shrugged. Jen, who had been whispering intently in Steve's ear, grabbed the man's arm and marched him off toward one of the officers. "There is something you need to know," she announced, and shoved Steve forward.

Officer Rick Austin looked up as they approached. The two women shoved his friend Steve forward and Steve stared at him with a deer in the headlights look. Uh Oh, Rick thought to himself. Part of his mind frantically tried to find a way to avoid Steve 'fessing up to whatever it was in front of everyone. Steve was one of those 'safe' people, just a big teddy bear of a man whose life revolved around taking care of his elderly mother and spoiling his dogs. Rick did not want to hear whatever it was that was putting that sheepish expression on the other man's face.

It was his duty, however, so he pulled out his notebook and called over one of the other guys to also listen, while Steve told a an embarrassingly misguided story about finding a foot.

"And why didn't you report it?" The other investigator asked, for what seemed like the tenth time, before Rick intervened. Steve got off with a long lecture about hiding evidence, disturbing a corpse, obstructing, etc. The man looked properly chagrined. Honestly, he was practically digging the toe of his shoe in the ground like a young boy embarrassed to be caught in a lie. Rick collected the information from the various members of the flyball team, a tall blonde with a chic haircut, another woman with long, dark hair and bangs, and the young black girl, all three somehow named some variation of Jennifer, a nervous young Hispanic named Luis, and then the other young woman who owned the dog that was found with the item, Sylvia. There was also the older couple, Dan and Donna, and, of course, Steve. Witness interviews would be properly scheduled at the police station later that week.

When they got back in the cruiser to drive off, his partner commented, "Why the hell didn't they report it? They should all be up on charges!"

Because Steve's an idiot, thought Rick.

"They are just normal people. They didn't know what to do," he said, instead.

"It's a freakin' foot!"

Rick couldn't help thinking his partner was throwing a lot of attitude, considering some of the stuff his kid got into, that he kept trying to cover up. That observation probably wouldn't help the situation, so he sighed and gathered his breath to try to explain.

"Exactly! Finding a foot in my back yard would throw me for a loop and I am a trained police officer. Even seeing that hand..."

"Yeah, I guess. Jesus, though."

"Yup."

Chapter 6

Recap

Sylvia twisted her way through the round metal tables at the coffee shop patio, looking for Jenny and Donna. In one hand she was carrying a canvas tote bag with picture of Cyrus jumping through a ring of fire on the front and holding Cyrus' leash in the other. The dog abruptly changed direction, winding the leash around her legs and she stumbled. The fall through the chairs felt slow motion. She dropped the bag, hit her elbow on a table, tipping it over, but still kept a death grip on the leash.

"Are you okay?" People started rushing toward Sylvia as she disentangled herself from the chairs and tried to shake the metal clanging of the dog's water dish against the concrete out of her ears. She gathered the dog toys, bags of treats, and water dish back into the bag and looked around for an escape from the attention.

"I'm okay, just graceful," Sylvia tried to laugh as hands reached for her to try to help. Fortunately, then she heard a sharp, light bark and spied the women and Flicker, the black tri Australian Shepherd staring at her in concern from where they sat at a table in the corner. Both the women and the dog had the same wide-eyed expression. She pulled Cyrus tighter, edged away from the helping hands of the other diners and made her way over, laughing at herself in what she hoped was a reassuring manner.

"Hi!" She said to her friends, hoping to make everyone realize she wasn't alone or in need of help, and get back on to a more comfortable dynamic.

"Sylvia are you okay? You're bleeding!" Jenny pointed at her elbow and held out a napkin. Sylvia took it and pressed it to the gash to stem the dripping. That's going to bruise, she thought. Long sleeves in summer suck.

"Yeah, despite Cyrus' assassination attempts."

Cyrus and Flicker wiggled hello and the leashes were clipped to the table. The restaurant had little rings welded to the patio furniture for that specific purpose. The waiter appeared, while Sylvia was busy untangling Cyrus from a chair. Donna must have ordered her something, because when she got the dog sorted out and sat down, a cup of something mocha latte like, topped with whipped cream was on the table in front of her. Donna just grinned at her confused expression.

"Dang, that was fast!" Sylvia took a cautious sip. It tasted creamy and sweet, with coffee undertones, much like pretty much any other item on the menu. In the background, she could hear the sounds of the tables and chairs overturned by Cyrus' tsunami of chaos being rearranged by the waiter and several customers.

"Acceptable?"

Sylvia nodded. "Thanks! Jenny, your hair is AWESOME today!"

Jenny laughed and preened at bit, flipping her wig's long, silver-tipped locks back over her shoulder. Sylvia thought the woman must have an entire wing of her house dedicated to her wigs. The white women on the team seemed to all have straight hair in some variation of blondish-brown, but Jenny, the only black woman, definitely made up for their lack of creativity.

"So," asked Jenny, "How did the interrogation go?"

"Interview," corrected Donna.

Jenny waved her hand dismissively. "Whatever, what did he want to talk to you about? Any clues? Is it Whacko Jacko's foot?""

Donna and Sylvia stared at their usually sweet and sun-shiney friend.

"Sorry, but, I mean that guy is crazy. I hope it's not his foot. That would be horrible. What about his dogs?"

"They won't know until they do the testing and autopsy it."

"You can autopsy a foot?"

They all paused a moment, sipping their coffee and cream confections and pondering the question. Jenny swallowed and continued.

"Well, I guess so. Anyway animal control needs to check on his dogs, just in case."

Sylvia nodded, and Donna spoke up.

"Jennifer says she is going to go over. She is concerned animal control will just euthanize them when they realize how bonkers they are. But, honestly, what else can they do?"

Sylvia shrugged, and offered, "It may be the kindest thing."

The neighbor's dogs, from what they had glimpsed through the fence and underbrush, seemed to be huge german shepherd and malamute mixes. They looked quite wolfy, and definitely were Not Nice.

There was another round of pondering sips. Flicker and Cyrus did the rounds, each collecting a precisely equal amount of ear skritches from everyone at the table, then they were placated with bully stick chewies from the bottomless bag of treats and distractions Sylvia had brought. You learned to be extra prepared with little cattle monster puppies.

"Anyway," Sylvia started. The other two immediately settled into attention. Coffee drinks were sipped and a huge blueberry muffin broken into chunks and shared as she told them about the long conversation at the police station. The police had picked and prodded, drawing out all the details of the trouble with the neighbor dogs. There was the constant fence fighting, and occasional breaking through or leaping over the fence.

"Did you tell them about the night Whacko Jacko's dogs dug under the fence and killed Steve's sheep?"

"That was awful! He said he just had to watch. Nothing he could do would stop them."

After that night, sweet, gentle, Steve had started going to shooting practice with Donna's husband. Sylvia didn't blame him.

"They already knew, but they asked me to tell them what Steve had said about it. I told them how he had described it and I told them that was why Steve had the gun. He was living in terror of those dogs killing more of his pets in front of him."

Sylvia caught her friend's expressions. "Uh Oh, should I have not told them? But they knew about his gun. He had it on him when they came out after the dog trapped us in the barn." Actually, Sylvia had made very sure he didn't have the gun physically in his hand when he talked to the police, but the existence of the gun had come out. Steve's firing of the warning shot had given her and Jen time to get to the barn and shut the door. Plus, the neighbors must have heard the shot.

"I don't think we should try to hide anything," said Donna, finally. "But, you didn't call the neighbor 'Wacko Jacko' to the police did you?"

Sylvia shook her head and then paused to snag a chunk of muffin. Ignoring Cyrus' pleading eyes, she quickly popped it in her own mouth.

"We need to figure out whose foot Cyrus was eating," stated Jenny, as Cyrus rested his head on her knee, looking at her adoringly, eyes flicking between Jenny's face and the bits of muffin on a napkin on the table in front of her. She fed him one, inspiring Flicker to also attempt puppy dog eyes.

"Chomp chomp," whispered Jenny to the cattle dog, causing winces from the other two women.

"It was Jonathan's shoe. Oh, God, you don't think it could really be Jonathan's foot, do you?" asked Sylvia. "Should I have said something?"

There was a pause. Donna met Jenny's startled glance.

"They are professionals. They will figure out who's foot it is. Leave them to it," Donna said. "I told them how he had been missing from the last several practices and we were beginning to worry about him. The officer said they would check it out, and I gave the contact information for his girl-friend."

This elicited a started pause.

"He has a girlfriend?"

"Yes, surprisingly."

"Eeeeewwwww"

There was a round of cackling. Apparently, Jonathon's personality had worn through the effect of his good looks for the women on the flyball team.

"Why can't any of us come up with anything nice to say about Jonathan? Are we such hateful people?" Jenny was crying. The sudden change in mood surprised the other two women.

"Because he is such an absolute ass," said Donna, as she patted Jenny's back. "I hope he is okay and that foot has nothing to do with him. But, Jonathan is a stuck-up asshat. He has caused so much drama and trouble for this team. Steve and I were trying to think of a way to send him off to trouble somebody else before he disappeared. Steve hates Jonathan."

"You didn't tell the police that, did you? Because I told them he had a gun and now you tell them he hated the guy," said Sylvia.

Jenny was looking at them both in horror.

"Jonathan is probably just fine, Jenny," Donna told the younger woman. Syvia tried to nod in support of Donna's assertion, but the memory of the blue Saloman interfered and the nod did not ring true.

They finished their coffees, gathered up the napkins and brushed the muffin crumbs off the table to be attended to by Flicker and Cyrus. As they tidied up, they reassured each other that Jonathan was fine. They walked the dogs across the parking lot to the pet store. The three women went up and down the pet store aisles with Flicker and Cyrus, practicing sit stays and recalls. They even tossed some toys in the cart for the blasted border whippets. Jenny was feeling better and back to her giggly, sassy self when they went their separate ways. She even found a squeaky tennis shoe for the dogs.

Before they left the pet store, Donna sent a quick text to Jonathan's girlfriend asking when a good time to drop off the toys would be. She had just gotten to her car when her phone dinged with an email notification. The girlfriend wanted to know if any of the team wanted to buy the border whippets. Donna expressed astonishment, double-checking, as Jonathan was so proud of those dogs and their prowess at flyball. It turned out that the couple had a fight about some business deal with her brother and Jonathan had stormed out of their house. She said she hadn't seen him since. Jonathan had been missing for quite a while. If he wasn't going to show up and take care of them, well she had never been fond of the dogs.

Donna sat on this for a half of a day, despite having just said they shouldn't try to hide anything. They had all said a lot of unkind things about Jonathan, and the idea that something might really have happened to him was rather appalling. Eventually, she couldn't let it sit any longer and Donna called Jennifer to pass on the message from the girlfriend about getting rid of the dogs and Jennifer told Donna she needed to contact the police. Donna tried to assure her that it was just a squabble. Unfortunate for the dogs, certainly, but pets are often uprooted when couples break up. Jonathan wouldn't have left them behind if he still wanted them.

"Maybe he just lost interest in flyball? It happens," said Donna. "We just need to find a good home for the dogs."

However, Jennifer explained to Donna that when she was trying to talk Jonathan into adopting the cattle dog puppy that Sylvia later adopted and named Cyrus from her rescue, she had him fill out an application and met the girlfriend, Shay Fount.

"So?" asked Donna, who wasn't getting it.

Jennifer explained to her "You need to contact the police and persuade them to talk to the girlfriend because Jonathan's girlfriend was the sister of the survivalist, crazy war dog breeding neighbor James Fount."

"Jonathan's girlfriend is Whacko Jacko's sister?"

"Yes. Which is why you need to call the police now that she is suddenly trying to dump Jonathan's dogs."

Chapter 7

Messenger

"This will be fun. NOT."

The two animal control officers sat in their van, looking at the house through the padlocked gate. Overgrown trees loomed blocking the sky. Brush underneath hid any pathway or access to the house. The greenery seemed full of unfriendly eyes.

"Maybe we can climb the fence?" Tommy was young, early 20's, tall, with brown hair shaved on the sides and long on top. His coworker, Lisa, was also in her 20's, a bit chubby, and had magenta hair with a neon green streak. They wore bright blue polos with Valencia County Animal Control logos. The van was full of empty crates, live traps and catch poles.

Tommy beeped the horn again, to no response.

"I can feel ticks crawling on me just looking at that," observed Lisa.

Beep, went the car horn.

Beep. Beep.

BEEEEEEEEEEEEEEP. This loud blare was not from the van. Tommy and Lisa looked around in surprise to see a portly older man with a grey neckbeard in front of the house across the street. He was dressed in camo gear and was sitting in the GMC pick-up with the door open, looking straight at them with his hand on the steering wheel, pushing and holding the horn button as hard as he could. The two animal control officers looked at each other as the horn screamed out a steady wail. After what seemed like a long time, the man let up on the horn. He stood there, glaring at them, ready to start again.

"Okay, then, I guess no beeping allowed?" muttered Tommy.

Lisa shrugged and rolled her eyes. It was her answer to a lot of stuff.

They waited, while the breeze rustled the leaves in the trees. Clouds drifted across the blue sky and the sun shone down. Lisa fantasized about a nice taco for lunch. Tommy reached for the horn. Lisa frantically signaled him not to. They had a hissing whisper of an argument over what to do, now. The man across the street eventually got out of his car and slammed the door. He pulled up his camo pants, adjusted his rifle, flipped off the animal control van and went back in the house. He slammed that door as well. No one had appeared at the house they were parked in front of, however. Birds resumed chirping. Insects buzzed. Tommy and Lisa admired the wild abandon of the greenery. Lisa thought about fish tacos and a sweet tea with ice cubes clinking in it. On a warm day like today, the water would bead up on the side of the glass. There would be a lemon slice.

"Where do they even practice in all that?" Tommy asked, finally.

Lisa looked at her coworker blankly.

"The flyball team? Didn't the dog attack people at a flyball team?"

Lisa pulled out a clipboard and looked at the papers.

"Flyball team was next door. To the south. Dog jumped the fence from over here."

"Oh."

Tommy and Lisa looked over at Steve's well-groomed yard and meticulously-trimmed trees. Sunshine danced and birds chirped. Then they looked back at the mass of feral greenery through the metal bars and rusted padlock of the gate in front of them.

"Nice neighborhood."

"Definitely a mixed bag, between the horse people, the rich hobby farmers, and the survivalist loons."

"Give me suburbia any day."

"Well, survivalist loon or not, we gotta tell him about his dead dog." Tommy got out of the car and eyed the gate.

"Don't get shot. Maybe we could just leave a note," suggested his coworker. Tommy was young and strong. He lifted weights at the gym almost every day. He did self-defense and Tae Kwan Do classes.

"Imagine it's your dog. Somebody shoots it and can't even be bothered to tell you. That's brutal."

"So's getting shot for trespassing. They seem to like guns around here. And I would be shooting my own dog if it jumps fences and try to eat people."

He shook off his coworker's worry and marched over to the gate, eyeing footholds to climb over.

"Besides, the owner would probably never see the note. It doesn't look like they come out this way often. It could be days before they saw the notice," Tommy said over his shoulder.

"If ever," muttered Lisa.

Tommy tossed his hair out of his eyes, set a booted foot on the bar of the gate. The bushes exploded with barking and growling. The dogs were huge. Tommy took a wary backwards step, spun and sprinted back to the van. He climbed in and slammed the door.

"Maybe we'll just leave a note," he said. Lisa nodded.

They drove down the street a bit and waited for the barking to subside. Lisa was fumbling through the various leashes and catchpoles, bags of treats and cans of cat food, muttering about tape or string to tie the note to the fence. While she was searching, Tommy spotted the mail truck making its way down the street. It would pull off the road next to each driveway to tug open the mailbox and shove in the letters and bills. The mail carrier would then adjust the little flag up before heading to the next driveway. The mail truck stopped at the house in question and delivered a bundle of items to the mailbox nestled in the bushes. The bushes, predictably, barked, but the mailbox seemed to be well insulated from doggy interference. Immediately after the mail truck left, the neighbor from 26 Cinder Lane, directly across the street, came out of his house. He was still decked out in camo head to toe. He furtively looked left and right, walked quickly over to the mailbox at the overgrown house and slipped an envelope out. He then quickly returned to his own house. The bush monster dogs announced their objections, but it was rather perfunctory and they quickly went back to their hidden lair.

Tommy and Lisa glanced at each other. Lisa nodded. Tommy walked as quietly as he could up to the industrial sized mailbox. Despite appearances, the mailbox was surprisingly easy to open. It was filled with Guns and Ammo, Survivalist Now and other magazines. Tommy tucked the notice in among the ammo magazines. Then, mission accomplished, the occupants of the VCAC van exchanged a celebratory high-five and headed back to town for those tacos.

Chapter 8

Packing for the Tournament

Sylvia's little Honda pulled up to the gate at Steve's house, windows rolled down to release Cyrus' excited howls. Steve had already pulled his truck up in front of the barn where the equipment was stored. Sylvia waved to him, then opened her car door and let Cyrus out to run up to the gate. Steve opened the gate to let the dog in and Cyrus sprinted off to join Steve's dogs racing around in the field out back.

"I hope you don't mind that I brought him. He needed to run off some energy."

Steve just chuckled and waved off her worry. "Get 'em, puppies!" he called out to his dogs. She glimpsed through the trees as the dogs slipped under the back gate and raced through the fenced field, barking joyously. Sylvia followed the older man over to the open barn doors and they looked over all the stuff to be loaded for the tournament.

"We should wait for Donna and Don," Steve said. "She has the list of what we need to bring."

"'kay. I am all for procrastinating," Sylvia agreed. They leaned, her against the barn and him against the truck, and listened to the cicadas buzz in the trees.

"Hey, how is your mom doing?" she asked.

"She's doing okay. Still sneaking Red too much people food."

Sylvia nodded. Donna and Steve had an ongoing banter session about Red, who was getting way too round. Donna kept badgering him to put the dog on a diet. Steve blamed his elderly mom for over-feeding the dog. Everyone knew who was giving Red all the treats that were turning him into a fuzzy beach ball with feet.

There was a pause, then Sylvia asked, "Have you heard anything from your neighbor? Is he upset about his dog?"

"No, nothing," said Steve, his worried gaze veering off toward the contentious fence line. "Honestly, I am a little nervous leaving my house for the tournament."

"You think he'll do something while you're gone?"

Steve just looked more worried.

"I have someone watching things and taking care of Mom, while I am gone," he said, finally, and visibly shook off his concern. "There they are! Hi guys!"

Donna and Don's long, maroon-colored car had appeared in the driveway. Sylvia grabbed the ever-ready ball launcher and headed out to the field to distract the dogs. Steve pulled open the gate so the couple could pull their car around Sylvia's Honda to park beside Steve's blue pickup. Donna got out, and bantered with Steve as her spouse maneuvered the car back and forth, apparently wanting to park with the tailgate toward the barn door. Sylvia was kept busy calling back dogs as they ran out the open gate and trying to grab them.

She eventually tackled Cyrus and held on to him, as Steve and Donna joked about "43 point turns." When the parking was completed, Steve whistled his dogs and closed the gate. Donna helped Sylvia climb off her frantically wiggling dog, and the younger woman brushed herself off.

The maroon car beeped and the tailgate began ponderously opening. Dan climbed out and walked over to join Steve. They nodded a greeting and then turned to look at Donna, expectantly.

"Well, Boss?" cued Steve.

Donna pulled out a sheet of paper and read off the first item: "Both flyball boxes."

Steve picked up the first cumbersome wooden device and staggered over to the truck. Sylvia reached for the other and Dan rushed over to help her lift it and carry it over.

"Hey, Steve, did you do this?"

"That's amazing!"

They all stopped to admire the custom-carved team nameplates on the flyball boxes. The two of them then got it lifted to the truck bed, where Steve had climbed in. He pulled it up towards the cab.

"Jumps," read off Donna, and they continued working their way through the list. Cyrus and Steve's dogs were a constant excited swirl getting in the way.

"Is your Mom's caretaker going to stay here," asked Dan, when they were waiting for Donna to double-check her list.

"BALLS!" Donna shouted, "Where are the balls?"

The required sniggering commenced.

"Ooops, they're still in the washing machine!" Steve admitted.

"Do they still need to dry?"

Steve confirmed that the tennis balls just needed a few minutes in the dryer. The washer and dryer were actually located in the shed. Steve had gotten them installed specifically for laundering buckets of tennis balls for the flyball team's practices and tournaments. Sylvia went over the machines in the back of the shed and lobbed balls from the washer to the dryer.

"I can put the tennis ball bucket in my car when Cyrus gets done running around," Sylvia assured Donna. "They should be done drying by then."

"He'll stop by during the day," She heard Steve say, answering the other man's question about his mother's caretaker.

"Will that be enough?"

"Yeah," said Steve, looking worried.

"We can put the stuff in the other cars, if you need to stay with her," offered Donna.

"Nah, it's okay. It's just over across town. I'll be home that night."

"Okay, if you're sure?" Donna folded up her list and started climbing in the passenger side of the maroon car. Dan pushed the button on the tailgate to close it.

"Yeah, the dogs will be here. They will stop anyone from bothering her."

Everyone's head whipped around.

"You think someone will harass her or something?"

"What's going on?"

"Wait, what? Is it Whacko Jacko?"

"No," explained Steve, making little quelling motions with his hands. 'It's the other guy, the one who honks his horn every time he hears the dogs barking when we practice. He's been doing little stupid things."

"Steve..."

"You need to talk to the police."

He just shook his head and refused to talk about it anymore. Everyone was subdued as they tarped and tied down stuff on the pick-up and reopened the tailgate on the SUV to readjust a few things. They confirmed the time they would meet up tomorrow at the field across town.

"You'll bring the ball bucket?" Donna asked Sylvia. Once again, Sylvia confirmed that she would. Dan and Donna left. The tennis balls were collected from the dryer and the bucket was tucked in the Honda. Sylvia collected her happily panting dog and said goodbye. She drove her little Honda back out the gate and headed home.

The next morning, the sun was sending timid, hesitant rays over the horizon that weren't strong enough to melt the dew off the grass in the soccer field that the tournament was in. There were people wandering back and forth from the parking lot hauling equipment and pulling carts loaded with crates. The rest of the team held onto their dogs leashes, standing in a circle around the loan ball bucket Sylvia had brought. They sucked down their coffees and worried.

Seven am and he wasn't there. The coffees were long gone. Donna repeatedly checked her phone for messages and sent him texts. Calls went unanswered. Hesitant worried conversations concluded that he must have been more worried about leaving his mom alone than he let on.

"She does have dementia. She probably shouldn't be alone."

"I know, but he just needed to tell us. We could have worked around it. But now we're screwed."

"The FurBallers say we can borrow their box and jumps. We're after them in most heats. And I had the balls in my car. It will be okay."

"He had the crates! It will SUCK. He should have talked to us!" Donna was livid. Everyone cringed and pussyfooted around her, which just made her more frustrated. It was a relief when the captain's meeting was called and she went off to that. After she left, they managed to find enough crates just from dragging the crates they used in the cars when traveling and doubling up a few dogs. Another team offered to let them share shade under their sun shelter. Jen picked up on Donna's mood and complained about Feist's measurement, talking about how unfair it was that he would have to jump 10 inches just because the judge couldn't measure properly.

During the course of the morning, Donna's texts to Steve got more and more worried. She assured him that they could work this out. She pleaded with him to answer. They were able to borrow a box from one of the other teams. Somehow, they made it through, though they were dead last in their division. The seed times were based on Jonathan's border whippets. The dogs picked up on the mood and ran out of the lanes, dropped balls, jumps were knocked over, and everyone was relieved when the long day was done.

"Are you going to go see Steve tonight?" Donna tensed at the question.

"No, don't. You need to cool off," said Jenny. Everyone nodded.

"It's just a tournament. There is a lot going on. And, his mother really needs looking after."

"But,"

"Just let it be, get through the tournament. We can talk it out with him after everyone recovers."

"I can't believe he would just leave us hanging..."

"We'll talk with him next weekend."

Chapter 9

Tournament Day 2

Sylvia's alarm went off at 5:30 next morning, sending Cyrus bolting off the bed for the back door. She rubbed at her eyes and tried to wake up. Throwing the covers back she thumped her barefoot way to the back door. "Mornings suck," she told Cyrus as she opened the door for him. He happily sprinted out to start a barkfest with the neighbor dogs. Fortunately, the neighbors were reasonable people who were still asleep on a Sunday morning when the sun hadn't even thought about sending a ray out over the horizon yet. So, the neighbor dogs weren't out in the yard, yet, and Cyrus was reduced to jumping at the fence over and over. Sylvia started up her coffee maker. The rumbling gurgle serenaded her as she dressed in jeans and a t-shirt with a picture of Cyrus mid-flight over a jump and the team name in a circle around it.

She sat at the table, sipping coffee out of a mug that read "Mornings Suck" and mentally went over the items she wanted to bring, as Cyrus raced around, knocking against the furniture and barking.

"You know something is up, don't ya? Yeah, more flyball today! You're gonna get to run! Yeah!"

As the dog danced around, barking, Sylvia tipped her head forward and started to cry. She should be excited! It should be fun! She had worked so hard. They had gone on four-mile walks several nights each week to build endurance. She had spent months teaching him how to bounce off the wall in a proper swimmers' turn. There had been so many challenges, with chasing the dog in the other lane, learning to bring the ball all the way back, all of that. He had learned so much. He was doing so well. It should be a triumph running with the main team, but it was just a mess. Steve wasn't there. They had to beg equipment from other teams. Everyone was all distracted and wound up.

And that foot that Cyrus had found had Jonathan's shoe on it. She knew it was Jonathan's shoe. Jonathan didn't have a tattoo, though, so it definitely wasn't his hand.

She had really wanted to prove to Jonathan that Cyrus was worth more than being thrown away at a shelter. Jennifer and her had planned and collaborated. For months, they had met for extracurricular practices to work through all of Cyrus' issues and bring out the potential that both Jennifer and Sylvia knew was in there, under the cattle dog crazies. Now, everything was falling apart. Today was going to suck. She didn't even want to go and face another long day of frustration and confusion.

The phone beeped with Jennifer's text that she was there to pick her up. Cyrus spied the car headlights through the living room window and began barkscreaming and frantically scratching at the window, so Sylvia wiped her tears, screwed her courage to the sticking place, and carried the crate and the flyball backpack to the door. "We're gonna have a good day, dammit!" she told Cyrus and opened the door.

"Hey, you wanna hit the coffee shop on the way," asked Jennifer when Sylvia climbed in.

"They're open?"

"Yup. I checked on the app. I'm gonna get everyone some mochalattewhatchamacallits to fortify us."

"Yay," said Sylvia, trying to work up enthusiasm.

There was a pause.

"Steve will be probably be there today. He just probably panicked thinking about leaving his mom alone. We'll help him. It will work out."

Sylvia nodded at her friends' reassurance.

"Cyrus actually did pretty damn good yesterday! He only ran out that one time, and he is hitting solid 4's. It would have shown Jonathan. Half the time, his damn dogs wouldn't even catch the ball."

"Yeah," Sylvia said, without conviction, and sipped her coffee.

"Just focus on doing awesome today. You worked hard for this. I know stuff is screwed up, but just focus on you and Cyrus. Okay?"

"Okay," Sylvia said, with a hesitant smile.

"And you bite them balls, you hear," Jennifer said to Cyrus in his crate.

"Bite 'em Bite 'em, Chomp Chomp Chomp" grabbing at the better mood, Sylvia joined the chant.

"Bite those balls," became the team's rallying chant that second day. The side eye glances from other teams that overheard it only added to the rally cry's power. Steve still did not show up nor answer any of Donna's texts or calls. Jonathan again graced them with his absence, but he hadn't been expected at this point. The FurBallers helped fill in with box loading and equipment, and the dogs all picked up on the raised spirits, dug their claws in and ran their little hearts out. Yes, at the end of the day, they were dead last in their division, but everyone still got toys at the awards ceremony. Jennifer won a crate at the raffle, and Jenny got a basket of goodies and toys for her dogs. Luis won a plastic trophy for his performance at Human Flyball. FurBallers, the host team, had really gone out of their way to make sure everyone had a great time and most everyone took home something fun.

Whether or not Steve was able to do flyball, they had to fix this. He was a friend. No, he didn't have the fastest dogs and they could run at a tournament without him. Steve was a good guy, though. He was so encouraging and seeing his kid-like enthusiasm was not something they were willing to give up.

"Plus, the way he hand-carved those team name plaques, you know he loves this. It doesn't make sense that he would just dip," said Jen.

"No, it doesn't. I've known him a long time. Yeah, his dog is too fat and slow, but he has always been there, encouraging new team members, making sure we had all the equipment, cheering everyone along. He does so much for this team. Something is really wrong, and we need to find out what it is and fix it," confirmed Donna. She seemed past the anger and well into worry.

In quiet conversations in the long downtimes between runs, the plan was formed for Donna and Sylvia to go to Steve's house the next day and help him unload the truck of unused equipment, and just talk with him to figure out what happened, and mend bridges. They would talk to him about his worries leaving his mother alone. Jennifer said her niece, who was a CNA, would be interested in staying at Steve's house as a caretaker on tournament weekends and maybe give Steve some respite care for his mother. Donna made a point to congratulate everyone on how well their dogs had done. Sylvia had even got on an honor board for a .000 start with Cyrus, and Flicker for a personal best line to line time. Flicker, Fiest, and the other dogs all had shown they got the game. After they had loaded up the crates and dogs back in the cars. Donna had delivered the thank you bottle of Jameson's to the FurBallers' captain for stepping up to fill in the gaps in the crew and equipment for the team. Then they stood by the cars, saying goodbyes. Donna announced her decision that Jonathan, and his glory-hogging border whippets were no longer part of the team. Then Donna climbed into her Maroon Lexus with Guiness and Porter and Dan, drove home. This left Jen, Jennifer, Jenny, Sylvia and Luis standing there.

"Whoa, she gets a bit harsh when Steve isn't there to balance her out."

"He does kind of balance her out a bit."

"We'll get it worked out with Steve and everything," assured Jen.

"I hope so," said Luis. Jenny nodded.

Everyone climbed in their cars and drove off.

"We'll get it worked out," Sylvia told Cyrus, before she turned the key. Cyrus, for once actually tired, just flicked an ear in his crate. Maybe there was a tail thump.

Chapter 10

A Little Help From My Friends

The maroon Lexus SUV made its way up the residential streets to Cinder Lane. Sylvia was riding in the passenger seat watching the patterns the streaming rain made running down the side window. Donna drove hunched forward, as she peered through the flood of water on the windshield, wipers going at the highest setting. The swish-swish of the wiper blades made a counter beat to Ella Fitzgerald playing through the car speakers. In the back seat rode Luis and Jenny, texting memes back and forth to each other. Today's hairstyle for Jenny was long braids. There were random indigo and hot pink braids mixed in. Sylvia wondered if it were actually a weave. At the corner, the flashy Arabian and his harem were tucked away in their respective barns, hiding from the rain. There was no howling. Cyrus had been left at home for this intervention.

With a slushy crunching through the gravel, Donna pulled the car up to the gate in Steve's driveway and put it in park. They all stared at the water streaming down the windows a few moments to gather their courage.

"So," said Donna, "Steve hasn't responded to any of my messages this weekend. He might be kind of worked up and upset. We don't want to gang up on him."

"No, of course not, but Luis is certified in home health care. He would be happy to help Steve take care of his mother,' said Jenny. Last night, after the tournament, Jenny and Luis had put forward their theory to Donna and Sylvia. They felt that Steve must have just been too worried about leaving his mother alone. While they all expressed frustration that he wouldn't just talk to them, it was a relief to have a potential understandable reason to latch onto.

Luis looked up, "Yeah, yes, of course." He put his phone down and continued, "Jenny and I were talking about it last night. He doesn't have to face this alone. It's very draining trying to take care of patients with dementia. Everyone needs a break."

"Whether or not he still wants to do flyball stuff," Donna clarified. Luis nodded.

"Yeah, no, whatever he wants on that, but he needs to know we're here to help. He's not in this alone."

"He's really done so much for this team and all of us. We need to support him."

There was another round of earnest nodding.

"Okay, sounds like we're all on the same page, then," confirmed Donna. Taking a fortifying breath, she pulled up her jacket's hood as she reached for the door handle. There was a rustling as everyone else followed her example and geared up as best they could for the downpour.

Sylvia had a moment of flashback, remembering Steve suddenly running off from practice to rush over to a frail, tiny old woman with a wisp of white hair tottering out the back door of his house. He had been so tall and large compared to his mother's delicate frame. There had been such excruciating gentleness as he chided her for not using her walker and shooed her back in the house. Her memories were interrupted when she spied a soggy cotton ball of a dog running out the driveway.

"Hey, is that Murphy?"

"Look! The gate's open!"

"Who's that? Oh, God, oh no, I think that's his mother!" They all poured out of the car. Luis and Jenny sprinted off in the rain to round up Steve's little fluffy Bichon while Donna and Sylvia ran toward the stooped figure wandering vaguely in the streaming rain. She was wearing the uniform of an invalid, pajamas and a robe and some now very muddy grippy socks. The woman seemed relieved to see them and didn't question their sudden appearance. She passively and wordlessly cooperated when Donna and Sylvia herded her back in the house. Everyone rushed around finding dry socks and a dry robe. Blackie and Red got up from snoozing by the fireplace to wander about, wagging and begging attention. The younger couple appeared with a soggy pile of white fluff and Luis took over gently encouraging the fragile senior to change into a dry robe and socks, then joined the frantic speculation about where Steve was and why he would leave his mother unattended. The old woman herself was no help. She did not utter a word and just took what she was offered and sat where she was told.

"His truck is still in front of the barn with all the flyball stuff in it."

"Steve is definitely not in this house." Luis had searched thoroughly while gathering up some dry clothes for Mrs. Henley.

"Where could he have gone? He must have run out for a minute."

"I think it was longer than a minute," said Luis as he slipped a cup in the microwave to heat up some water and found a packet of herbal tea. "She looks dehydrated and off her meds."

There was a pause.

"She's endangered?" Donna's question was very, very deliberately specific. Everyone froze.

"Yes, I think so." Luis' answer was also very deliberate.

"We need to call 911." Sylvia started to draw breath to contest it, but looked at the old woman shivering in the chair, frantically clutching the tea Luis handed her. Her eyes were glazed and unfocused. She looked so excruciatingly vulnerable. Luis pulled out his phone and started dialing.

During the wait for authorities, they exchanged worried speculation about where Steve was.

When the driveway was full of flashing lights and paramedics loaded Steve's confused mother into an ambulance. No one else had any luck in getting answers from her. The officers kept asking each of them, one by one, and each of them when questioned, assured them that Steve was far too conscientious to ever abandon his mother. No one knew where he was. It was Luis who first mentioned the ongoing issue with the neighbor across the street, the one who honked his horn and played a siren to object to the barking during practice.

"You don't think..." Jenny started to ask, then froze, staring at the officers.

Of course, the officer insisted on following up that thought, and drug out the entire story of the feud, the minor vandalisms that Steve had mentioned, his ongoing worry that it was escalating. The emergency responders promised to check it out. Sometime during the questions and search of the property and evacuation of Steve's mother, Jennifer had appeared. She joined her teammates to stand in a confused huddle, watching with big eyes. Eventually, the driveway in front of Steve's house cleared of emergency vehicles. Jennifer, Jenny, Luis, Donna and Sylvia were left looking at each other.

"You don't think we got him in trouble by calling" asked Jenny.

"He was already in trouble. He would never leave his mother like that. Something's has happened to him." Jennifer's voice was decisive until the last statement, when it started wavering. Her gaze was drawn to the screen door with the view of the back yard. "William," she stated suddenly and marched out the back door. Jenny and Luis looked confused.

"William is her ex. The homeless guy who lives in the woods at the back of these properties," explained Sylvia. She had pried that info out of Jennifer when she was trying to figure out why Jennifer wasn't on board with pushing Steve to report the foot. Sylvia realized that didn't really explain Jennifer's calling her ex's name and taking off in this moment. She didn't have the impression Jennifer and William were on good terms, or much of any terms, to be honest. So, Sylvia followed after her friend, the rest of them trailing behind.

Fortunately, the rain had let up. It was muddy and wet, but the water wasn't pouring down on them, except whatever was running off the tree leaves. They formed a half-circle behind Jennifer as she confronted a tall, long-haired man a short distance outside Steve's back door.

"He didn't tell me he would be gone this long. He just asked me to keep an eye on Mrs. Henley during the day Saturday and Sunday while he was at the tournament. He was supposed to be back, I tell you!"

William's long brown hair was pulled in a braid down his back and a bushy beard covered the lower half of his face. He was tall and lanky, dressed in several layers of murky-colored clothes. For a homeless person, he was surprisingly put together. His brown eyes were wide and intense as he spoke to Jennifer. Those eyes flickered around, noticing the rest of them as he continued explaining. According to him, Steve would frequently ask William to house-sit, keep an eye on his mother and the dogs, when he had to leave his mother alone. William would disappear when the caretaker came for the regular visits. Steve had arranged with William to watch his mother this weekend Friday evening, just before he headed over to talk to the neighbor across the fence about the dog that was shot.

"Wait, why would he trust..." Jenny's voice tapered off, not sure how to ask the question in a socially acceptable way.

"He knew him from when we were together," said Jennifer.

"We used to visit when he was adopting all the dogs, Blackie, Red and Murphy, from Jennifer's rescue. He knew, and after," William paused, not wanting to say it.

"After you discovered meth and I threw you out."

"Yeah. After that, he caught me sleeping in the woods. I was too crazy to stay in his house, but he left me a tent and stuff, and helped me kind of crawl back to sort of normal. He tried to find me jobs, but every time, as soon as I started to get kind of together, I would go back to drugs."

William paused to swallow, not meeting anyone's eyes. Then he continued. "Every time I relapsed, he would help me come back. Eventually, I realized that I just needed to not be around people, so I just stayed here, in that tent. I owed him everything. So, I helped him any way I could, just as long as I didn't have to be around people." You didn't have to be around anyone but a demented, non-verbal, vulnerable old lady. Sylvia decided to keep that suspicious and unkind thought to herself.

"So," asked Luis, "If you were watching Steve's mother, where were you?"

William's head whipped around to face Luis' accusation.

"His truck was still here! It never left! I thought he was here!"

Steve had alerted William and William had known Steve would be gone. The understanding was that William would be on duty when the truck left. It usually would work out just fine, except this time, the truck never left. It was still there, parked in front of the barn, full of flyball equipment. So, where was Steve? Where would he have gone without the truck? It was a rural area. There were no stores or restaurants. The neighbors were Whacko Jacko the survivalist and Horn Honker. Neither were the type to invite one over for a cup 'o tea. There was no one he would have gone visiting. So, they were back to the question that had been haunting them all weekend: Where was Steve?

"Wait," said Sylvia, "You said he went to talk to ummm," she hesitated with the wording, not remembering the guy's name. 'Wacko Jacko' seemed disrespectful. And, at this point, she kind of suspected there had been a tattoo on one of his hands, back when it was still attached. What was going on here?

"Yes, he was going to go over there," William nodded at the overgrown house next door. Everyone's heads turned to contemplate the ominously dripping, secretive overgrowth on the other side of the fence. "I tried to talk him out of it. Told him he should leave it to the police. I thought I had him convinced, but, where else would he have gone?"

"Did he take his gun?"

"How would I know?" William asked. "I am just guessing that's where he went. Anyway, it wouldn't matter if he took his gun? Steve would never shoot anyone."

Chapter 11

Visiting the Neighbors

Where was Steve Henley? It was a question that Officer Rick Austin was very interested in, as well. Rick knew Steve. They had grown up together in this small town and still practiced together at the shooting range, and talked smack about each other's political views and sports teams. Rick had known Mrs. Henley since fifth grade. She had treated him like a second son. When he broke his arm during basketball practice, it was Mrs. Henley who loaded him in her car, and driven him to the hospital the next town over. It was Mrs. Henley he had to face and stammer apologies to when he and Steve were screwing around, throwing rocks and broke the window. Her decline had happened mostly in the background. Steve took such conscientious care of her to keep her in a familiar environment, with a familiar routine. It was shocking responding to the call and find her soaked, frightened, and confused.

You can get very disillusioned doing police work. People do very shitty things, sometimes from malice but most often from greed, stupidity, and laziness. The rest of the day after that responding to that call, Rick had tried to tell himself that was what happened with Steve. There had been rants to his partner about how disappointing it was that Steve had abandoned his mother like that, just run off, apparently. There would be charges, of course. The dogs and animals they were able to pawn off to the care of his flyball friends. It didn't settle right, though. This just didn't feel like something Steve would do. Steve Henley had been one of the nicest guys he had known. He would not do this. So, what the hell happened to him?

Rick tried tracking down that homeless guy that Steve had befriended. Steve had been sneaky about it. Sneaky was never a good sign. Rick had learned to pay attention to the things people were sneaky about. He had remembered the guy had developed a meth problem after his kid died. A lot of times, drugs were contagious. People got into drugs when their family or friends were into it. Once people got into drugs, they lost themselves. Steve was one of the good guys out there. He was someone you could trust. He definitely wasn't the kind to disappear and leave his demented, helpless mother to her fate. Drugs would have made it believable and that homeless guy had drug offenses on his record.

Rick and his partner had gone back to 25 Cinder Lane after the friends had left, and beat the woods looking for William James. They found his camp. There was an expensive looking tent that there was no way he could have afforded, and a solar generator, and other camping gear that must have come from Steve. They confiscated it, but no sign of the man himself. They hadn't found any drug paraphernalia in Steve's house, which was a good sign, but they did at that little campsite. Returning later with a K-9 unit they were able to track him down and bring him in. Hours of intense questioning drew from the man anger, fear, confusion, but not one hint that Steve Henley was in any way, ever, involved in drugs. Rick was left with no answers and released the guy when he realized he was getting nowhere. Thinking of Steve, Rick bought the guy a hamburger to eat as he waited for the person William had called to drive him back to his little hidey hole in the woods.

Next, Rick followed up on the suspicions about the neighbor across the street. The man was so fond of honking horns and being a general asshole. However, being an asshole wasn't illegal. It could certainly lead to illegal activities, however. They drove up to his house at 26 Cinder Lane and knocked on the door. The door was answered by the wife, a woman with thin greyish blonde hair in a utilitarian bob, and a face of someone who was just waiting for whatever next is going to hit them. She was quietly unsurprised when they introduced themselves. They showed their badges and asked about her husband. Not questioning that her husband was being sought by the police, she just let them in and quietly led them into the living room, where a conservative news channel blared on the tv. There was the expected amount of attitude, but her husband's bluster quickly crumbled when he realized they were serious, and they brought him in for questioning.

He shamefully confessed that he was responsible for several small vandalisms and general assholery. They definitely weren't best buddies, but nothing he said gave them any idea where Steve Henley currently was or what might have happened to him. When the wife came to pick him up, Rick could overhear her asking him what it was all about. She tut-

tutted in concern when her husband told her that Steve was missing. "Steve is such a nice person," she said. "I really hope do he is okay." Apparently, she was unaware of, or deliberately overlooking, her husband's petty harassment hobby. A wife of a man like her husband probably had to overlook a lot.

Rick and sat in his cruiser, stopped in the driveway of 25 Cinder Lane. The house was quiet. No dogs came out to greet him. He stared at Steve's backyard, at a loss what else he could do.

Where was Steve? Was he okay?

Chapter 12

Crusader

"Cyrus!" Sylvia called, and sprinted away from him, down the back aisle at Pawdimonium. She and Jennifer had decided to meet in the pet store to work on recalls. When the cattle dog just reached his owner, Jennifer called his name and ran the other direction, frantically waving and honking his duck toy. Cyrus slid to a halt, whirled around to go chase after, his leash clanging behind him. Almost, her reached her, when his owner called him back. This time she caught hold of the leash and reeled him in. Jennifer walked up to her, panting a bit from the exertion and smiling.

"He's doing really well, not even looking at the toys in the aisle!"

"Should we try it in the treat aisle?"

They started walking down to toward the front of the store. It was so nice that Jennifer could always be counted on to find time to help with training Cyrus. Sylvia hoped it wasn't left over guilt from when Jennifer had placed him with Jonathan and Jonathan had dumped the cattle dog at a shelter. It wasn't Jennifer's fault Jonathan was a manipulative ...

Just then, Jennifer's phone rang. She pulled it from her pocket and checked the incoming number. Looking confused, she pushed the button and held it to her ear.

"Hello?"

Sylvia watched an entire Broadway musical of emotions flash across her face.

"William? Why are you...?"

Confusion appeared. Then outrage.

"What!?"

There was a long pause, while Jennifer listened to her phone and Sylvia watched her brows draw down and her body tense up.

"They had no right! I will be right there."

Jennifer crammed her phone in a pocket and stormed toward the door. A parade of people and young dogs from the puppy classes practicing heeling on leash in the main aisle parted like the Red Sea before her. Donna had her occasional snippy moments, but Jennifer was a goddess of wrath when she found cause.

"Jennifer? Is everything okay?" Fortunately, Sylvia was able to rouse up her dog and catch up with her before Jennifer reached her car, because they had actually driven there together, in Sylvia's car. The woman looked like she would rip the door off. Sylvia got the destination from Jennifer and was treated to a long, enraged, rant about police misconduct and overreach, all the way to the station. She was then left to wait in the car with Cyrus while Jennifer went inside. Sylvia had never been to a police station in her life before she was brought in for the interview about the hand. Or was it the foot? There were entirely too many stray body parts involved. Anyway, she was back again, but at least she wasn't inside. Hopefully, this would be the last time. She and the dog rocked out to golden oldies while they waited. Queen was playing "We are the Champions" when Sylvia spotted Jennifer marching out of the glass double doors of the police station, followed by a very subdued-looking William. Sylvia was glad she couldn't hear whatever Jennifer was yelling as she snatched the fast-food hamburger bag William was holding from his hands and threw it in the trashcan right outside the doors.

"I'm sorry! I had no one else to call," she heard William say as Jennifer pulled open the rear door of the Honda and practically shoved him in with Cyrus. Sylvia could feel the whole car rock. He had to move quickly to fold his tall frame into the little car. Cyrus and he stared at each other, transfixed.

"Ummm, Hi puppy?" said William. Cyrus looked at Sylvia for guidance.

"It's okay, Cyrus. You can say hi."

William offered a tentative hand, that Cyrus sniffed.

"I am not angry at you, William" said Jennifer as she furiously yanked the passenger door open and dropped into the seat. The poor, abused Honda rocked again.

Sylvia thought she was pretty angry at someone. She hadn't seen Jennifer this enraged since she found out that Jonathan had dumped Cyrus at the shelter, when Sylvia had first joined the team. There was a tense silence. Sylvia wondered where she was supposed to drive to. Maybe Steve's house?

"Are you okay? Do you need anything?" she finally ventured to ask the man, as Jennifer sat in the seat, staring out the window and fuming.

"Kinda hungry," he admitted, then glanced uncertainly at Jennifer.

"Okay,"

They ended up at a Subway sandwich shop, trying to speak quietly to not draw attention, as Jennifer drew the whole story of his ordeal out of William. Sylvia noticed the mother and two young children at the table next to them quickly gathered up their food and left. The staff were listening intently behind the counter. When Jennifer had worked through expressing her outrage at the police's treatment of him and minorities and the poor and people in general, the conversation turned more toward the details of what they asked him about.

The police really wanted to find Steve, especially Officer Austin. They believed his disappearance was connected to the hand and foot that had been found. For hours, they pushed William, saying a man's life was at stake. William kept telling them he did not know where Steve was and he really, really wished they would go look for him, because something wasn't right.

"That foot," William said, "they figured out who it was. They did DNA."

"It's Jonathan," said Sylvia, remembering the teal Saloman shoe with purple laces.

They both looked at her, startled by her certainty. Sylvia had been having nightmares about that foot in the shoe for a while. It was a little mystifying why no one else was making the obvious conclusion. Now, maybe they would get on with figuring out what was going on.

"Yeah," confirmed William. "They told me the name, Jonathan Frost, and I recognized it from when Jennifer was interviewing people, trying to place that dog." He nodded at Cyrus, who was curled up under the table, hopefully not being noticed by anyone else in the restaurant. Actually, after Jennifer's earlier rage, Sylvia didn't think anyone was inclined to mess with them.

William continued his story. "I told them about that, but that was all I knew about him. How did you end up with the dog?"

"You recognized Cyrus?"

"Yeah, he was a cute puppy. Jennifer had him fostered at Steve's house for a bit."

Jennifer explained the story of Cyrus being dumped at the shelter and then adopted by Sylvia and showing up at flyball practice. William muttered a derogatory name for Jonathan under his breath and received a tense nod of confirmation from Jennifer. Sylvia reached down to scritch her dog's ear and the thought suddenly hit her. It was true. Jonathan was really dead. She remembered his endless array of spandex runner's outfits he wore to every practice. She and Jenny had been all flustered by this dark blonde man with the chiseled features and perfectly toned body in high end spandex. "I'm married, not dead," Jenny had whispered to her when Donna had teased the younger women about being all fluttery around the new guy. Then, Jonathan had opened his mouth and they all got over him very quickly. He did like to buy the team high-end pizza and beer at tournaments. When they came up for the design of the new team shirts, he had been so excited, insisting on it being reworked, over and over, to get it absolutely right. She wondered about his border whippets, that she could never remember the names for and seemed virtually indistinguishable except for their meticulously color-coded gear. His whole identity was invested in those dogs, and now his girlfriend was looking to pawn them off for whatever cash she could get. She hoped they found a good place.

Sure, Jonathan had done some pretty questionable stuff. She remembered him trying to teach Jen's dogs to crouch for measurements. He seemed to go through dogs like tissues, breaking them down with constant, repetitive boxwork practice and excessive drills. The dogs had no apparent relationship to him and ran to anyone who held a tug. She remembered him throwing a fit when one kept dropping the ball, and then the next practice it was gone. The dog had been replaced immediately with a different dog, with gear in a slightly different theme color. Jonathan never mentioned that dog again. One of the team members had dog sat his dogs once. The dogs weren't even housetrained. Jonathan never participated in the pictures with Santa or other just for fun team things they did with their dogs. The border whippets did nothing except flyball. Now it looked like they wouldn't even have that. They would just more overbred, high-drive, poorly-trained dogs used up and dumped into the rescue system.

Maybe the word William had muttered to describe Jonathan was appropriate, after all.

They finished up the meal, and Jennifer insisted on grabbing a tent and some camping gear before they pulled up to Steve's house and sent William back to his woodland realm.

Chapter 13

Found Him!

. They knew the foot was Jonathan, and, honestly, no one seemed that upset, except for a feeling of guilt about not being more upset. Even Jenny, the most soft-hearted of them, seemed to be just going through the motions of grief. But Sylvia heard no mention of speculation about who the hand belonged to until she was driving back from Cyrus' obedience class. She was driving down the highway, windows down, Cyrus hanging his head out getting high on the smells in the wind. The news was playing on the radio. When she heard "investigating multiple suspicious deaths at 27 Cinder Lane" she nearly swerved off of the road.

She yanked the steering wheel to wrench the Honda back in the lane. A red jeep swerved around her, horn blaring, woman in the passenger seat flipping her the bird as aggressively as she could manage. Sylvia quickly found a spot to pull off to the side at the off-ramp to an overpass. Wheels crunched in the gravel of the roadside. Turning up the radio dial and shushing the dog, she took deep breaths to calm her heart rate as she listened as the announcer described the finding of a detached foot and then a hand. The foot was identified as belonging to Jonathan Frost, who had been missing for several weeks, and the hand was identified as James Fount, the property owner at 27 Cinder Lane. It really was Wacko Jacko's hand, she thought. The report also noted that Steve Henley, another local landowner, was still missing.

Missing isn't dead, she told herself. It wasn't looking good, though. What was going on? The news moved on to the next report. Collecting herself, Sylvia eased her car back into the roadway and continued on her way.

Rick Austin was getting pretty worried, too. As Sylvia was pulling her Honda off the highway to listen to the story on the radio, he was pulling his cruiser up in front of the rusty, padlocked gate at 27 Cinder Lane. Two other cruisers pulled up behind him. Across the street the man who was fond of honking horns whipped open his door. He had a bullhorn in one hand. It must be what he was using to make the siren noise his neighbors kept complaining about. He spotted the cruisers, met Rick's hard stare as the policeman got out of his vehicle. Apparently, the obnoxious neighbor changed his mind and went back inside. The curtains twitched, but there was no other response from Horn Honker.

Rick nodded to himself in satisfaction. That neighbor wasn't going to be an issue today. He then walked around to the back of his vehicle, opened his trunk and pulled out the bolt cutters.

"I thought there were supposed to be dogs?" It was one of the other policemen, looking nervously at the overgrown brush.

"Oh, crap, yeah! Weren't they eating..." confirmed one of the others. The bolt cutters broke through the lock, and the bushes erupted in snarls. There were some swearing and quick pops of gunshots and then the snarling stopped.

"God, they are fucking huge!"

There was no response to the shots. Rick led the way past the corpses of the dogs and towards the house. Everyone was tense, backs to each other, guns out, looking every direction for more dogs to come flying at them.

Over and over, as they inched toward the front door, one of the officers would call out announcing they were the police, there to serve a warrant. But there was no response. There was no response to the knocking. There was no response when they got the ram and knocked in the door. There was no response as they moved from room to room, clearing the house, kicking aside heaps of ammo magazines.

There was a room dedicated to dusty fitness equipment and another had an astoundingly varied gun collection. Lots of things no upstanding citizen should ever need displayed in that gun room. The meth lab was in the garage. One of the officers let out a whistle of appreciation at the racks of high-end lab equipment in the fully-finished custom set up. Usually, it was a burner and some trashy pots in a barely standing porch or shed. When Rick reached the back door, he realized with some chagrin that it was unlocked. Rick saw a well-used looking path from the door to a row of large, chain link dog runs.

"Looks good, then. We'll leave you to it." The rest of the policemen chose that moment to leave Rick and his partner to document the house and look for clues. Their jangling equipment belts and thumping footsteps marked their progress back through the house. Soon, the sound of car engines starting up and tires in gravel announced their departure. A creepy quiet descended over the house.

Rick stood there, looking at the kennels, reflecting that this must be where all the dogs had spent their lives, until a week ago. It occurred to him to wonder if there might be more dogs. His eyes went down the row, confirming they were empty, when he saw one in the run on the left was still occupied. A huge, black, wolf-like dog, climbed to its feet. Malevolent amber eyes were fixed on him. Fortunately, that gate was shut. The other runs had holes dug under the sides or open doors. It looked like the latches had been deliberately wrenched open. Each run had an igloo-style dog house in them. The one with the dog still in it had something, it looked like a piece of scrap plywood, blocking the doorway to the dog house. Rick stepped closer, and heard the low warning growl. He noticed the bits of animals and bones scattered in the runs. Not just animals. That looked like...

"Uh Oh, I think we found them!"

"Found what?"

"The rest of those guys."

The other policeman abandoned what he was doing and hurried over to stand with Rick, looking at what was lying in bits in the dog cages. He swore softly while the black dog in the last cage continued to growl, low and with intent. While they waited for animal control to come take the last dog, they wandered through the open runs, setting up crime scene tape.

"Here's a shoe. Teal Salomon. Size 11. Looks like a match to the one on that foot."

"An Apple watch."

"Watch your step! Is that a Glock?" The policeman hopped up in the air to avoid stepping on the uncleared weapon.

Whenever they moved toward the last cage, the black dog in the cage snarled and lunged at them. Rick spotted the litter of puppies she was protecting, hiding in a heap behind the doghouse. When animal control came, Rick persuaded them not to shoot her. They caught her with a loop. She was drug out, and the wiggling, snarling puppies were removed and hopefully headed off to a better life.

When the commotion settled, Rick heard something. Some scrabbling from the dog house. A muffled voice. The plywood blocking the door was wiggling. His companion reached for his gun, but Rick stopped him. He moved closer. It did not sound like an animal, Rick held up his hand, shushing the others.

"Listen."

"What is that?"

Suddenly, Rick rushed forward and starting pushing and tugging on the plywood blocking the door. He got it to move a bit and a hand dropped out. It was still attached to a person and, miraculously, the person was still alive.

Rick grabbed a hold of the shirt the arm was wearing and dragged the person from the tiny dog house. It was amazing that such a large man could have fit in there. Ignoring his partner's questions and commands, Rick guided the man over to the cement steps leading to the back door and helped him sit down. The man began working to move his cramped limbs, understandably giddy with relief at being out of that doghouse. It was Steve. He wasn't in good shape, but better than he should be considering he had spent a weekend and a day trapped in a dog house hiding from a very pissed off mama wardog.

While he was sitting in the ambulance, waiting to be taken away, wrapped in an aluminum blanket and sipping water from a ridiculously overengineered sippy cup, Rick asked him how the hell Steve had ended up in that situation. Steve explained about going over to ask his neighbor to round up his dogs. He described knocking on the door and shouting with no response. He was shooting his gun in the air to scare off the dogs until he got to the back door of the house and spied the mother dog trapped in the cage without water. There had been a streak of hot weather and it was obvious to him that there was no one around, and she had the puppies. They were just babies. He had found the plywood scrap and thought it would work to protect him when he went into her cage with some water and food. It worked, kind of, until the door had closed behind him. The doors were carefully engineered to prevent the dogs getting out. Spring loaded automatically locking latches and guard plates prevented any chance of getting it open from the inside. Momma was pissed. He took the only shelter he could find and crawled in the dog house.

"You are a soft-hearted idiot," Rick told his friend. Steve nodded in agreement. Honestly, it was just such a relief to know Steve was still who he thought he was. He assured Steve his mother and his dogs and his cat were being taken care of. "So was the Momma Dog From Hell and her spawn." Steve then let himself be taken to the hospital to be looked over.

Before he was taken away, Steve handed Rick his gun. He'd had it on him the whole time. There were still bullets in it. Rick's partner was laughing about how he should have just shot mama dog and he would have been fine. Steve didn't even think of using it on the mama dog.

"Of course he wouldn't," Rick told his partner as they drove away. "It's Steve." His partner rolled his eyes and muttered about idiots. Valid, but Rick was smiling, his whole face so much more relaxed than it had been for days. He felt so much lighter. It was good to remember that sometimes, people didn't have deep, dark secrets. Sometimes, they were exactly who you thought they were.

Chapter 14

Mama Mia

"They found him?"

"He's really okay?"

Jennifer nodded confirmation.

"Wait, Steve is back? Where the fuck was he?" Jen could be blunt, when called for.

Jennifer made shushing motions with her hands and her fellow flyball teammates quieted a bit, glancing guiltily around the hospital waiting room. There was a middle-aged lady in a wheelchair sleeping over in a corner. A stressed family fussed over a teenage boy who was enthralled in a video game on the I-pad, ignoring the blood running from his face and a cut above his eye. Several homeless people huddled in a group in the corner. Sprinkled about were several confused and apathetic looking old people.

Jennifer had been watching Steve's dogs, so she was the one who received the phone call to come to town to pick him up. She had been quick to pass what she knew on to the rest of his friends. Everyone in the flyball team had rushed over to the hospital in the next town over because they wanted to see, in person, for themselves, that their friend was okay.

An aide rolled a wheelchair out the double doors. Steve smiled a chagrined smile when he saw all his friends. "Hi guys," he said. "You didn't have to all come out."

He waded through the mash of greetings and interrogations about what happened as paperwork was signed and he was rolled out to Donna's Lexus. He wanted to pick up his mom on the way, but a call to the care home led to assurances that she was doing fine.

"It's late. She's fine. She's probably in bed. Let her be tonight," advised Donna. "Take a night to rest and recover and get ready. Maybe get groceries and stuff. Luis wants to talk to you about helping out."

"You've been taking on too much with her," said Luis, from where he was riding in the back.

Steve started to argue and assure them everything was fine, but they eventually persuaded him that he had been through a lot, and it was best to just rest tonight. Steve seemed relieved by the decision and rested his head on the headrest of the seat, letting Donna drive him home. Jennifer and Sylvia met him there, with takeout, some groceries to stock the fridge, and his pets. They all shared pizza and beer.

"Well, we should be heading out and letting Steve get some rest," hinted Luis. Sylvia and Jenny were quick to gather the dishes and load them in the dishwasher. They were a bit confused by the faucet in the sink.

"Where is the handle?"

"I think there's a sensor."

"Where?"

They waved hands around the faucet until water came out. The dishes were rinsed and countertops wiped. They put the leftovers in the fridge. Fairly quickly, Steve was left to relax and recover after his ordeal. Everyone headed to their respective homes knowing Steve was enthroned his leather lazy boy recliner with his dogs, a plate with slices of meat-lover supreme overboard pizza, a beer, his plugged in phone and the tv remote all within easy reach.

They left him to recover the next few days, other than a quick text now and again, checking in.

"Do you want help unloading the flyball stuff from the truck?" asked Dan, Donna's husband one day.

"Did the cat come out after we left?" asked Jennifer.

"Let us know if you need anything," said Sylvia.

"Remember, we're here to help," said Luis and Jenny.

Other than those quick daily check-in's, there wasn't much heard from Steve. He had been through a lot. They had agreed to give him time and, also, there was a bit of uncertainty where he stood with flyball and things.

Steve was the one who sent the group text reminding everyone about flyball practice in the morning Saturday. The cars collected at 25 Cinder Lane. Dogs rushed out and joined the happy barking pack in the back field. Jumps, flyball boxes and crates appeared in the field and formed the two lanes. Steve had to fend off concerned looks and awkward hugs, then they settled into the practice routine, women wrangling excited dogs and the guys gathered to the side, talking about guns and guy stuff. Dan was drafted to boxload, which left Luis talking with Steve. The conversation turned to how his mother was doing back home.

It turns out Mrs. Henley wasn't back home. Luis gently prodded to find out if it was something to do with her being left unattended, but it wasn't that.

"She didn't recognize me," said Steve. "At all. I went to pick her up and she kept asking the caregivers who I was and looked scared." The big teddy bear of a man was trying to keep his voice level. His eyes glistened.

"I should never have left..."

"No. Don't do that," scolded Luis. "It happens like that. That's dementia. It sucks. It so sucks. But it didn't happen because you left. It was the disease."

Steve nodded. "That's what they kept saying."

"She's doing okay, otherwise, though, at the home?"

Steve nodded.

"And," Luis paused an awkward moment, "It's okay her being there?"

Unfortunately, working in healthcare had given Luis a lot of insight into families' struggles when a member needed memory care. It was expensive. Over and over families were financially devastated and having to make bad choices from bad options. The healthcare system in this country, especially for the old and disabled, was horrible. Steve had done so much for their team. They would find a way to help him through this. He was such a nice guy.

"Yeah, she seems happy. She looks well cared for. They have all sorts of programs to keep her entertained."

"You can afford it?" pressed Luis, "Long term? It's realistic?"

Steve assured that, yes, it was well within his means.

"It's good then. You are doing good by her."

"Yeah, I guess. I just thought I would be the one taking care of her."

"You are doing the best thing. The people there are trained how to keep her calm and make her feel safe and as empowered as possible." Luis assured him. "She's lucky she has you."

Later, Luis confessed how relieved he was to his wife, Jenny.

"It was such a relief to know that Steve and his mother would be okay. Honestly, the hardest part about working in healthcare is seeing people get financially destroyed."

"People who do that work need to get paid," Jenny said. Her husband nodded. "And it's not like they get paid enough as it is," she continued.

"But, it is so hard on the families, financially," he said.

"Steve is okay. He's loaded."

"You have no idea how much money it takes," her husband said. He thought of all the commercials targeting seniors with things like reverse mortgages and fake medicare to strip them of every single asset and bit of cash they had earned through their lives.

"It will be okay, sweetie." She rubbed her husband's shoulder and wished she could erase the haunted look in his eyes. Jenny knew Luis loved working with people, helping them heal, and he was good at it. But she was pretty certain this, how the cost of healthcare was handled in this country, would drive him out of the field. She hoped he would hold on long enough to pay off the student loans.

Chapter 15

Time Passages

T ime passed. Long summer flyball practices got colder and briefer. The fate of the Evil Momma Dog who had held Steve hostage for a weekend in a doghouse was iffy. She was not a creature bred and raised for domestication.

"I'll take her," announced Steve.

"Steve, no ,,," Jennifer was shaking her head in dismay

"Where else is she going to go? William used to feed them, when James went on trips or whatever. He can help me."

"Embark shows she is 59% wolf, Steve. No. Just no." Jennifer wasn't a fan of that idea, either.

"Besides, according to William, he just lobbed chunks of raw meat in the cages. It wasn't like they weren't above chomping on him, given the chance." Luis joined Jennifer in trying to talk sense into their friend.

"Wolves are just, like, wild dogs."

"These aren't, I mean they haven't been raised right. He was wanting war dogs. He raised them to be as vicious as he could get them.

Jennifer apparently abandoned the conversation and was typing on her phone. Then Steve's phone rang. Waving their

93

argument aside, he looked around and found the phone on a table.

"Hello?" he answered.

"Hi Rick! What's up....Yeah, no, no. How did you even know about this?" Steve shot an accusing glance at Jennifer. "Hi Officer Austin," she called out with a smirk. Steve glared at her, then at her gesture, handed her the phone. "Would you explain to your friend that there is no way in hell he is adopting that damn dog that tried to kill him for three days? 'Kaythanxbai." She handed the phone back to Steve and went back to messing with her phone. The volume was turned so high that they could all hear the voice on the phone repeating what Jennifer said to Steve, verbatim. The rest of the flyball team stood around Steve's living room as his police officer friend continued to lecture Steve about how he should listen to the nice rescue lady about how wolves weren't good (or legal) pets. Dan, Donna, and Luis were distracted by a football game on television. Jen and Jenny were taking turns playing ticklebug with Steve's fluffy little white dog, Murphy.

"You don't want to be any Wolfie snack, do you, Murph?" Jen asked the little fluffball. Sylvia heard her phone ding. She glanced at the message, caught Jennifer's eye, and gave her an affirmative nod and thumbs up.

Meanwhile, Steve was resorting to playing dirty on his phone call with Rick, pointing out that "Officer Austin" wasn't what Jennifer usually called him. It was usually something a bit more derogatory.

"Yeah, well, I have called her things other than "Nice Rescue Lady," responded Rick. "Name calling aside, we both agree that you are not adopting that damn dog."

Steve finally capitulated.

"Well, what's going to happen to her, then? It's not like she's going to be adopted at a shelter. It's not her fault!" Steve said.

"She's in a rescue's boarding kennel until the pups are weaned. They know how to handle her, at least short term, and the puppies are young enough to be rehabilitated."

"And long term? What's going to happen to her? Is anyone going to rehabilitate her?"

Jennifer showed him the link to the wolf sanctuary in Colorado she had found. "We'll take her up there as soon as the puppies are weaned," Jennifer said, nodding at Sylvia. "She will get to be what she was meant to be, instead of in a cage or terrorizing a suburban neighborhood. Okay?"

Sylvia added, "As awful as it was, when his dogs came over and killed your sheep, you never want to be the person on the other side, having to stand there and say 'sorry my crazy wolf dog ate your pet in front of you."

There was a weighty pause. Finally, Steve nodded his acceptance of the plan, and everyone gave a sigh of relief. Monday, two weeks later, Jennifer picked Sylvia up in her rescue's transport van. Bad Momma spent the entire drive up to Colorado staring Sylvia down and growling.

"Whoa, Is that an Impact crate?"

"Yup."

"Pricey."

"Yup. Steve donated it to the rescue. Said Bad Momma should ride in style."

Sylvia was mesmerized by the yellow eyes glaring at her through the ventilation holes in the crate. It with all the crash testing they do on those crates, it should hold her.

"Steve is a good guy."

Jennifer nodded in agreement.

"And a rich, good-hearted guy can do a lot of good," said Jennifer.

"Thank you for finding a rescue for her," Sylvia continued. "I was terrified that Steve would end up with her."

"No way that would happen. She is high enough content to be classified as a wolf. Pet wolves are prohibited."

"Oh, good. Pet wolves sound really dangerous."

Sylvia paused for a moment, then continued.

"But they allow pet chihuahuas?"

"Go figure."

They continued driving down the road, switching drivers every few hours. Sylvia warily asked if they should get Bad Momma out to go potty. Jennifer looked at her and cracked up.

"No. Absofuckinglutely not."

"'kay, then."

They traveled through the desert, crossed the mountains at the border, then wound through forests. Sylvia could see slivers of a lake through the pines. Jennifer turned off and they drove on progressively more rugged roads. They were down to a winding dirt road punctuated by boulders. After a particularly dramatic thump, Sylvia asked, "Are you sure your van is up for this? Don't break an axel or whatever."

"Yeah, Steve would have to buy me a new one!"

"Don't do that. Don't be that way, please."

After a pause, "You're right. I am sorry. I didn't mean it. I value Steve as a friend, not a money pit."

"It's just been a long drive with Bad Momma," Jennifer continued.

"Are we almost there?"

Sylvia was looking kind of squirmy.

"Why? You have to pee? We could pull up to a bush."

"Nah, if Bad Momma can hold it, so can I. Sisters in solidarity"

"Solidarity of very full bladders."

"Here we are!" They were facing a 20-foot-tall chain link fence peppered with No Trespassing and Danger signs. Jennifer stopped the van and put it in park. The sanctuary had a front-facing education experience center where people could commune with the wolves. This part was for the more non-communal type wolves.

"Where is that number?" Jennifer muttered to herself as she scrolled through her phone. Apparently finding the contact, she stabbed at the screen. It was on speaker phone, so Sylvia got out of the vehicle to walk around and stare through the fence. "Here Wolfie Wolfie," she whispered.

No wolves answered, but she heard the sound of an approaching car. Soon, a white Ford Transit van pulled up to the other side of the fence. Several tall men dressed in flannel and camo got out, carrying catchpoles. They looked like they worked out, muscles everywhere. A middle-aged woman unlocked the padlock and they opened the gate. She waved Jennifer and Sylvia to drive through, then closed the gate behind them.

"Stay in the vehicle," they were instructed. The men opened up the back, grabbed the crate with hay hooks and carried it to the white transit van. Bad Momma expressed opinions. Some paperwork was handed over and then the gate was opened, Sylvia and Jennifer were waved back through. The gate was shut behind them and the white Transit van disappeared back where it came from.

"Alrighty, then," said Sylvia.

"I guess that's it," said Jennifer. It was nearly dark, so they drove to the nearest town, found a McDonalds and a Motel 6. Sylvia scrolled through the channels trying to find something other than Naked and Afraid on the television, then called Donna to check how Cyrus was getting along. Donna assured her that Cyrus was being an angel, an obvious lie. Sylvia let her know that she would pick her dog up tomorrow afternoon.

Bad Momma may have legally been a wolf, but her puppies apparently had a shepherd/malamute daddy and were released to rescue to be placed once weaned. One of those tiny black puppies was soon running around Steve's yard and became part of the greeting committee every flyball practice. Midnight seemed a friendly thing, a little black puff with a pink belly and needle-like teeth that doubled in size every time you blinked. Donna quickly squashed Dan's tendency to buy inappropriate toys for the Midnight after she caught him ordering a fake foot squeaky toy on Amazon. She gave it to Cyrus, instead. Sylvia was not thrilled, though Dan and Luis were very entertained. Jennifer worked with Steve to conscientiously socialize the puppy and find appropriate outlets for his prey drive. However, the little baby war dog was banned from flyball. He would probably be too big to do a box turn, anyway. Jennifer spied the flyer from the local shutzhund group on Steve's kitchen table one day.

"Please don't teach that innocent puppy to bite people," she said to Steve.

"It's in his genes! Doesn't he need an outlet?"

"Not for attacking people! Just find stuff that uses his brain and energy."

Steve agreed to go with scentwork, instead. There was a collective sigh of relief.

Fortunately, the weather was nice for the Christmas barbeque. The dogs swirled around, playing tug with stuffed Santa and Reindeer squeaky toys, while Dan and Steve manned the outdoor barbeque grill and the rest of the team arranged various potluck dishes on the picnic tables. As Guiness, Donna's border collie, wandered about, Sylvia and Jenny watched her, thinking puppy thoughts.

"When will you know if she's preggers?" Asked Jenny as she gently patted the dog's belly.

"The ultrasound is next week." Donna told her.

They all looked at the dog, evaluating.

"I hope she took, this time," Jenny said.

"I think so. She already looks fatter," said Donna.

"So does Red, and we know he isn't pregnant," observed Sylvia.

Steve rolled his eyes at the comment and returned to plotting with Dan about when they would sneak out the dismembered foot squeaky toy for the dogs to play with.

The burgers were ready and the women each got one, and some jello salad, chocolate cake, broccoli slaw, or chips and dip and whatever else of the sides appealed to them, and gathered at a table looking at pics from a documentary about the day-to-day development of puppies in the womb. They chattered about the sire, and the health testing, and all other aspects of the potential puppies. Dan, Steve, and Luis rolled their eyes and talked about football, while sneaking chunks of hamburger to the dogs. Guiness may have gotten a bit extra, but as Luis explained, she was eating for 7. Steve thought from the way her eyes glistened pleadingly that it must be closer to 12. Dan said the dog had told him in confidence that it was 23. And they were very hungry.

Next Tuesday Dan lifted the ever-fatter Guiness into the car and drove the border collie and his wife to the vet. After a brief time in the waiting room, they were shown to an exam room. The chatty vet rolled in the portable ultrasound and they all stared at the screen. With a squeal, Donna announced spotting the first black circle with the tiny blob of a puppy inside. The vet assured them she was certainly pregnant, but thought maybe 5 or 6, rather than Dan's assertion of 23.

"Could you email us the ultrasound?" Donna and the vet went through the images, trying to find one that showed as many of the little black voids with a dot inside as they could. "Five, right?"

"Or six, but it is really just too early to tell. Sometimes they hide, or are reabsorbed."

Donna and Dan nodded, but they had promised to send Sylvia and Jenny the first baby pics of their puppies. Dan even circled one and told Sylvia it was her split faced black tri with ticking. Donna picked which little dot in a dark circle was Jenny's red and white. In any case, whatever color they turned out to be, there were black circles on the ultrasound with little jumping beans in them, so Guiness would not be running in the New Years' flyball tournament. Donna contacted the host team and their entry was quickly converted to pairs and singles.

"Too bad about Cyrus," said Dan.

His wife shot him a startled glance and asked, "What happened to Cyrus?"

"Sylvia's been working so hard. This was supposed to be his debut as the official start dog on the team."

"She'll be okay. We'll do the spring tournament in Las Vegas and he can debut there. He needs a bit more practice anyway," Donna was distracted, thinking about her pregnant dog.

Dan took off his ever-present baseball cap and smoothed his thinning hair back against his head. He wasn't sure, but the tournament was in a month, and Guiness would be waddling around like she had swallowed several bowling balls. Between that and losing the border whippets, there just weren't enough dogs for a team. Sylvia would have one of Guiness' puppies to console her, soon. And, there was the Spring tournament.

Officer Rick Austin sat in his patrol car and thought. He tended to spend a lot of time doing that. Rick was happy his friend was found safe and sound. He was glad Mrs. Henley was in proper care. The homeless guy, William, seemed to have retreated back into his woods and wasn't causing any trouble. He might be involved in some way, but he obviously wasn't the lynchpin of any big plots.

There were still two dead people.

"One more dead meth cooker survivalist whack job is an improvement," said his partner.

"Maybe, but another one will take his place. And there is that other guy."

"Jonathan Frost? Nobody seems to miss him much, either. Even his girlfriend got over it pretty damn quick."

That was certainly true. After losing her brother and boyfriend, she had packed up, sold the dogs and disappeared like a puff of smoke. Nobody seemed to care. Everyone was just moving on with things. A life, with all the ambitions, fears, secrets, and dreams, could be erased, just like that. Everyone around just adjusted and kept on keeping on.

"Yes, but they are dead. And they had help getting that way." Rick finally pointed out.

"The warrant came through for the recordings on the ring cameras at the house. Let the computer guys go through it. When we can look at that, maybe it will help with some answers."

"Oh, right," said Rick. "I need to get that taken care of."

"What do you need to take care of? The computer crime guys will do it?"

Rick waved him off. He needed answers for his own peace of mind.

"Another thing – that girl, Sylvia?" said his partner.

Rick looked at his partner in confusion.

"Do you know why she left her last job at the university?" the man asked.

"No?" Rick replied.

"She used to work in the psychology department. Doing data stuff. Anyway, they were needing some volunteers for students to evaluate brain scans. There is some theory about the parts of the brain that are more or less developed for like psychopaths or whatever. She volunteered and they scanned her brain. She fit the model. Everyone kinda freaked out about it."

"Sad. I am surprised they publicized it. Seems like that should be protected information."

"It was students learning to administer the test and evaluate it. They talk. It got around and things got awkward for her. So, she left."

"She should probably sue the university."

"Yeah, well," his partner continued, "She is apparently not normal. More like Ted Bundy or something. I want to know what she is up to."

Rick didn't respond. After a pause, the other policeman continued.

"It doesn't seem right, having people like that just out there."

"People don't kill people because of brain scans." Rick said. "They kill people because they are afraid of something, want something, or something like that."

"She wants her dog to run flyball! This Frost dude was taking all the spaces on the team."

"So did everyone else on that flyball team."

"But they aren't psychopaths!"

"She isn't a psychopath. She has a slightly different brain scan."

"A psychopath brain scan!"

"Show me means, motive and opportunity. Not brain scans." Rick held up his hand to hold off his partner and clarified, "means, motive and opportunity more so than anyone else on that team. Then we will talk."

"Those dog people are crazy," his partner muttered. "And she is certified psycho or something."

"Psychos don't have pet dogs. You are on the wrong track."

"Maybe."

Chapter 16

Gratitude Trap

"You don't have to live like this."

Sylvia stood in the woods in the rain, talking to the tarp covered heap that was William's camp. Steve and Jennifer stood shivering beside her. Why am I the one stuck talking to him, she asked herself. They know him better. Apparently, she was the designated speaker.

"Come to the house. Steve has a room for you."

Silence responded.

"You're cold and miserable. You don't deserve this." Jennifer said.

"You know I do."

"Why would you say that?"

"Amy."

Jennifer sighed in frustration.

"Please come to the house. Get dry and warm. No one deserves this."

"It's safer for everyone. It's the only way to keep safe."

They argued back and forth, but made no progress, and ended up trudging back through the wet woods to the house, leaving William behind in his self-imposed exile. They huddled around the fireplace in Steve's living room, drinking hot chocolate and trying to dry out. Sylvia looked over and noticed that the water running down Jennifer's face was tears. She was crying, silently. Sylvia started rubbing the other woman's back consolingly.

"I know it's hard seeing him like this," she said.

"You think," asked Jennifer, her voice heavy with sarcasm.

They listened as Jennifer vented about William. She told them the whole sad story of their relationship and the drowning of their daughter, Amy. They heard about William's descent into drug use, getting him into recovery, and the vicious cycle of recovery and relapse until they broke up and he ended up living in the woods.

"It's so hard, when a child is lost tragically. It breaks a lot of couples up. The grief just isolates them from each other." Sylvia's words were an accurate observation, but they weren't soothing.

"No. Not grief," Jennifer argued. "William and I were arguing. He thought I was cheating. He was bathing her, had her in the tub, but followed me out the door, screaming at me. After he went back in the house, she was floating in the tub, dead."

"He was so utterly devastated. He called me. I didn't answer, at first, but eventually I did, and then rushed home. He was irrational. She was still floating in the tub. I was in shock, and called 911 and when the police came. They thought it was me. That I was one bathing her. That I stepped away and panicked."

Her companions looked at her, wordlessly, for several minutes.

"Why?"

"I was in shock, robotic. William was the grieving parent. I was an emotionless drone."

Her friends were silent, unsure what to say.

Jennifer waved it away, wiped her tears.

"It's late. It's done. But, yes, William is racked with guilt because not only did she die on his watch, I was the one who was prosecuted. I even went to trial. Fortunately, I wasn't convicted, but it was excruciating. And he got the luxury of grieving and being consoled. So, he punishes himself, heaps the coals on his own head to make up for it. And, I have to watch."

Guilt traps you like that, thought Sylvia, to herself. It really didn't serve much useful purpose. The harm had already happened, and guilt just magnified the damage. That was one of those thoughts she knew by now to keep to herself.

"Let's go, let Steve get some rest. Come on Sylvia," Jennifer briskly slapped her hands on thighs, rose grabbed her keys and stood at the door, waiting for her friend. She wouldn't meet anyone's eyes.

"All I do is rest! Really, I am fine. Why do you all keep babying me?" protested Steve.

It was a tense ride with Jennifer driving Sylvia back home. She refused to utter another word about what she had just told them, eyes resolutely fixed on the rain-soaked road glimmering in the headlights. The passing lights occasionally caught Jennifer's spikey blonde hair and illuminated the stark expression on her face. Sylvia was left with her thoughts. It was hard not to be a bit angry that William had somehow been thrust through the barrier of anonymity that homelessness overlays on people. There didn't seem to be anything that could be done to help him, so, like Jennifer, now they all were trapped by guilt watching and knowing he was huddled out there in the rain and cold. It was a relief to be dropped off at her home. Cyrus distracted her with wiggles and the contents of the trash can artfully strewn through the living room, when she opened the front door.

However, once Sylvia had cleaned up the mess, and took the dog for a late-night walk in the fading rain to settle him for the evening, her brain kept circling around on the tarpit of guilt and gratitude that bound William to his ex. He was desperate to make it up to Jennifer for stealing her child and her opportunity to grieve for her child, and gratitude that she didn't rat him out to the police, because he would be under scrutiny that he would never be able to withstand once they looked at his history of drug abuse and other petty crimes that the homeless incur by existing. And, a similar sucking trap bound him to Steve. Steve kept rescuing William, every time he relapsed into drugs. Steve made sure he was fed, had a tent and blankets and food, and ran interference so the police didn't hassle him. William would do anything for Steve and Jennifer.

Absolutely anything.

Steve was trapped with a neighbor from hell. He'd learned not to involve the police because there were no real consequences for the neighbor and then the man was just more pissed and hostile towards Steve. Jennifer made no secret of the fact that she was so angry with Jonathan. The feud had even escalated to a lawsuit. Jennifer was blackballing Jonathan in the rescue network and several dog groups on Facebook. Jonathan had talked of filing a lawsuit against her for defamation. Donna and Steve had talked him down, but the threat hovered out there. That was part of why Donna had been willing to put up with him on the team and give his dogs prominence.

Neither Steve nor Jennifer were the type for vigilantism. They had too much to lose. But William had already lost every single thing he cared about in this world, even his sense of self-worth. He was so desperate to be of some value to them, to anyone, to balance out the badly out of balance flow of favor and debt he was mired in.

Now Steve's problem neighbor and Jennifer's enemy were gone. Poof.

And, William would do anything for them.

How could she think this way? Was she really that prejudiced against homeless people?

Syliva decided she should stop thinking. Cyrus was subjected to a bath and blow dry. She tried mopping the kitchen and shampooing the living room carpet, and a hot shower to wash the train of thought away. She added several puppy toys and an enclosed pop-up ex-pen to her Amazon cart. There was a book on alien abduction stories to give her mind something else to work on. Just stop thinking about it, she told herself.

Chapter 17

Jonathan's Backstory

Donna sat in the interview room at the police station. Her eyes were big as they flickered around, noting the blank greenish-gray walls and complete lack of furniture other than the utilitarian white laminate table and three army green chairs with the kind of plasticky fake leather that squeaked like a whoopee cushion fart whenever you shifted your weight. The two police officers came in. They sat down opposite her at the table, wincing at the noise the chairs made. Officer Austin seemed all gray bristle. His hair bristled in a short buzz cut. The stubbly beginnings of a beard grew out of his square face. The other was young and boy-band handsome, with inky black hair and dark, emotive eyes. Donna thought to herself how she would be glad when this investigation was done and she could go back to blissful middle-class ignorance of police stations and interview rooms.

"Here's your coffee. Would you like sugar? Cream?" The packets were dropped on the table next to the cardboard cup holder with the three steaming cups.

"Thank you," said Donna. Her straight grayish brown bob framed huge blue eyes with the deer in the headlights look.

Rick Austin and his partner introduced themselves and made awkward small talk, as they dumped various additives in their coffees and stirred them in. Finally, Rick took a tentative sip, winced, and said, "Ms. Perry, we just wanted to ask you some questions, get to know a bit more about Jonathan Frost."

Donna froze and stared at them. Rick had to fight the urge to reach over and pat her hand reassuringly. Instead, he waited to see what she would offer. It was one of his go-to interview techniques. When nothing appeared to be forthcoming, he decided it was time to prompt.

"How did you get to know Mr. Frost? I understand he moved here from Texas?"

Donna took a fortifying sip of coffee and swallowed. She winced and slid it the cup further from her. She did not want to say anything that might drag Jennifer, or, well, anyone, further into this mess. Gathering her thoughts for a moment, she responded.

"Yes, he was in a flyball club there called Fur Fleet. They were one of, if not the, top flyball teams in the country."

The officers nodded, encouragingly.

"Well, Jonathan ended up moving here..."

"Do you know why?"

"Why he would move from one of the top teams in the country to our little backwater?"

The officers nodded. Apparently, they wanted some doggie drama tea. Much better that they focus on that and not the mess with Jennifer's rescue.

"Well, there was a bit of a scandal. Jonathan ran on a team called Fur Force One. They were making the records and then breaking them to set new records..." began Donna, warming to the subject. The police officers just nodded a lot and took notes as best they could.

"Apparently, the team wanted some really fast, short dogs to be height dogs." Donna noticed the blank looks on the policemen's faces. "Height dogs set the jump heights for the team. It's based on the shortest dog. Actually, there is a bit of debate about measuring. One venue measures the dog standing, the height at the withers, the other measures the length of the bone in the front leg..." Donna noticed the policemen shuffling in their chairs. Maybe she was getting to far into the weeds with this. She continued, "The shorter the jumps, the faster and easier it is for the bigger dogs. There is usually one little, hopefully fast, dog on each team to make it easier and more competitive for the rest. That's what Jen's little Jack Russells are for our team." Rick nodded encouragingly. His partner was tapping his pen on the notepad impatiently.

"Um, so we're kind of a casual team. We're just in it for fun, maybe four tournaments a year. But Jonathan and his team were all in. Very competitive. Tournaments every weekend and they host the Big Bling Bash tournament and hold seminars and stuff. Instead of just finding a little, fast dog, they like to cross border collies, who are fast and driven, with something smaller. There are trends. Borderstaffies were a thing for a while, and Borderpaps. Even Jonathan's border-whippets are a sportmix that is trendy in flyball. But you don't really know what you will get..." Donna heard the police officer clearing his throat and exchanging a glance with his partner. Before they could speak up and control the conversation, she dragged herself back to the topic at hand. "Ummm, anyway, Jonathan bred one of his female border whippets to the Jack Russell owned by another teammate, and a litter of potential borderjack height dogs was born. Jonathan wanted the pick of the litter, but he wouldn't pick. Eventually, when the puppies reached ten weeks, the team distributed the puppies among various members and called it good. Jonathan was pissed. He fought and fought trying to get the particular puppy he had decided would be best away from the team captain's 10-year-old daughter. The daughter was in love with the puppy, that she named Noodle, and her parents were not going to rip it away from her to give to someone who had a reputation of going through dogs like Kleenex." The policeman seemed a little more attentive now.

"Well," continued Donna, "Jonathan sued his teammates to try to force them to hand over the puppy. He thought that since his dog was the dam, the mother of the litter, he was entitled. He lost the suit, but this brought out that the Jack Russell had been used for breeding sport mixes, which was very much against the contract with the breeder the dog had been purchased under."

Rick caught his partner's attention and rolled his eyes. His partner chuckled. Donna continued with her story. "The wife of the Fur Fleet's captain was a veterinarian. She had been forging paperwork for the teams' dogs. Health certificates, vaccination records, pedigrees, and she had made false certificates indicating the Jack Russell was neutered. That was the only way the original breeder of the Jack Russell was willing to sell to a flyball team."

Rick's pen had stopped scratching on the paper as he wrote notes and he was just looking at her in amazement.

"How did you find all this out?" asked the other man.

"Gossip at tournaments. I talked to some of his old team members and confirmed it."

Donna continued.

"I don't know how familiar you are with breed clubs?"

"Not very," admitted Rick.

"Well, a lot of them don't really like the whole designer dog sport mix breeding thing. They often sanction or even revoke the registration of dogs that are used that way."

"So, Jonathan caused trouble for the breeder of the Jack Russell the team bought the height dog from?" Rick asked.

Donna nodded in confirmation. "Yes, you are doing really well at following the doggy drama. It gets better. The breeder of the Jack Russell was banned by her breed club for participating in the breeding of sport mixes and sued for breach of contract. There was a whole scandal about hung papers. The veterinarian wife lost her license and ended up in legal trouble. A whole legal mess ensued for pretty much everyone on the team. The club was disbanded by the flyball organization, and Jonathan was blackballed in Texas. So, he moved a few states over to find a team far removed from the mess and try to rebuild his reputation. I gave him a chance, but he was on the last leg of it with our team and then this happened."

"Why was his on the last leg with your team? More 'doggy drama'?" asked Rick.

Donna certainly seemed to have warmed to the subject. The woman was sitting relaxed in her chair, gesturing and nodding for emphasis.

"No, he was just an asshole. He got on my nerves. Not a team player kinda dude. And then there was the mess with Cyrus."

The detectives looked at her, expectantly. If they were dogs, Donna thought, the two policemen would have pricked their ears and tilted their heads. Repressing her smile at the thought of the interrogators as inquisitive puppies, she continued.

Donna told them the whole story of how Jonathan had adopted Cyrus from Jennifer's rescue when he first came. "He didn't want that cattle dog."

"He was into designer sport mixes, not rescues," said Rick.

"Yeah. He was just trying to get in good with the only flyball team in the area." Donna, distracted, risked another sip of her coffee and continued.

"But, as soon as he was let on the team, he dumped that poor puppy at a shelter. Jennifer wanted to kill..." Donna abruptly recollected where she was at and to whom she was talking. Rick could see her thoughts spinning, trying to figure a way out of that particular turn of phrase. She fiddled with her coffee cup but couldn't make herself actually drink from it.

"So, Jennifer was pretty pissed at him?" clarified Rick.

"Well, we all were. It was a pretty crappy thing to do. And he didn't tell anyone. Until Sylvia found that dog at the shelter and showed up at an open practice, none of us knew. He should have just sent him back to Jennifer's rescue if it didn't work out."

There weren't any more dramatic revelations after that, and Donna was soon escorted out and sent home. The police officers went over their notes, trying to understand what Donna had called 'doggy drama.' Rick ended up summing it up by concluding that dog people were crazier than meth addicts.

"But, are they killers?" asked his partner.

"I don't think so, but," Rick couldn't figure out how to continue.

The following weekend, Rick pulled his personal vehicle up to the gas station. He unbuckled and went into the gas station store, telling himself to act civilian. It felt strange to not being in his uniform. The line was long. It was lottery day. Eventually, he got up to the counter and muttered the number of the pump and stuck his card in the reader.

"Hey, can I get a receipt," Rick asked.

The clerk, a wiry old man, mumbled and pushed some buttons on the register.

"Shit, hey, where is the receipt paper?" he asked his coworker. The other clerk was going back and forth with a person at the other register trying to identify what type of Fireball they wanted to buy. There were so many options lining the wall behind the counter.

"It's out?" the other clerk asked.

"Yeah."

The coworker rolled her eyes and both started rustling around behind the counter and in the cupboards underneath.

"I can't find it," said the clerk helping Rick.

"I'm sorry, dude, but I need it for work."

The clerks looked at each other, restrained themselves from rolling their eyes, and then tried searching through the drawers under the counter, again. Rick could hear people behind him in line sighing and muttering.

"Maybe there is some in the office?"

"I can't believe they let us run out of receipt paper!"

"Listen, it's okay," said Rick, figuring he could just take the hit for a tank of gas. By this point, though, they were on a quest and there was no stopping the clerks. The old man headed back to the office while the other clerk was emptying the drawers behind the counter, and customers started abandoning the line to head out the door.

"Hey, can I get my booze, already?" This was from the customer that the other clerk, a young woman with turquoise-colored hair, had been helping.

"Sorry, Hun, here you go," the clerk said. The customer left with their purchase and the rest of the customers moved to that line. The young woman quickly rang them up and got them out of the store. Rick was left standing there, with her awkwardly staring back.

"Sorry, I just need it for work."

"No worries, Hun. Not your fault. We shouldn't have let the paper run out."

A pause. Their eyes accidentally met, then veered off, so the clerk was staring somewhere off over Rick's left shoulder, and Rick was admiring the array of liquor on the back wall. Seriously, how many different flavors of Fireball could there be? Oh, it looked like the others were various knock off's, copycats, and off-brand flavors.

"He'll find it in a minute," said the clerk, to the display of buzz bombs by his left elbow.

Rick nodded an awkward acknowledgement to the bottles of Bubblegum Blast.

The clerk had a pen in her hand that she started tapping against the cash register in a rapid rhythm.

"Where are you headed, anyway?" This she asked while actually looking at him.

"Catron Fairgrounds. I think my phone's map program is lost, though," Rick said, distractedly looking out the store window.

"Probably. You can't really trust those apps on these back country roads. So, why are you headed there?"

Rick took a moment to adjust himself to being on this side of the questions.
"There is an event there, um the Balls to the um Wall..."

"Oh, yeah, the dog thing! My sister's in that! Well, her dog is, I mean." The woman giggled at herself. The old man clerk reappeared, triumphantly cradling several rolls of receipt paper. He made his way back around behind the register counter. While he loaded the machine, the young woman tore a section of paper off one of the rolls and drew a map. The receipt printer chattered and Rick was handed the receipt.

"Thanks," said Rick.

"No problem, officer." Rick did a double-take as both clerks smiled and waved him off.

So much for my undercover skills, thought Rick.

He followed the sketchy map while the voice in the GPS of his phone kept instructing him to "make a legal u-turn." Eventually, it started chanting "recalculating" and then gave up entirely. By then, there were colorful signs posted to trees and signposts reading B2TW and Flyball!, and arrows made of tennis balls glued together and stuck to signposts.

Rick pulled through the gate and arrived at the parking lot of the fairgrounds. He found a spot lining up with one of the rows of vehicles, and sat for a moment, casing out the place. The gravel parking lot was full of SUV's and RV's, many of which barked continuously. People were walking dogs everywhere, most holding the leashes to multiple dogs at once. Rick watched in admiration as a slim young woman guided a fan of seven different black and white dogs out the door of the building, through the crowds of other dog walkers, to a spot off the end of the parking lot. Her hair was braided in several different orange and green braids and she was wearing a t shirt with some type of logo spelled out in tennis balls. The curving path she effortlessly cut through the mass of people and dogs reminded him of a sailing ship negotiating rough seas. She reached a grassy spot at the end of the parking lot with her entourage and told them all "go potty." The dogs all obediently began lining up with tufts of grass, or turning circles, apparently preparing to comply.

The police officer uncomfortably playing civilian unbuckled his seat belt and stepped out of his car. He tugged uncomfortably on his NM Tech T-Shirt and pulled on his Isotopes baseball cap. So many people and so very many dogs. They were walking everywhere on the grassy fairgrounds. Pop up sun shelters dotted the grassy swaths, edged with metallic sun shade clothes and full of dog crates. He followed the sound of barking toward a large exhibit building. Signs drawn with markers featuring tennis balls and pawprints on either side of the doorway announced the flyball tournament. He waited for a pause in the stream of excited dogs and people and ducked into the building.

The barking was even louder inside. It echoed off the cement floors and the surfaces of the walls and ceilings. It seemed like everywhere there were groups of people holding leashes to herds of straining and barking dogs. All the dogs were absolutely frantic to get to the lanes in the center. Rick watched three black and white border collies running in place like cartoons. Their paws got no purchase on the floor. The dogs were held in place by a teenager holding the leashes who was paying no attention to the dogs. The teen was talking with a group of others about random numbers, 3.59, 4.02, 4.5. The four lanes in the center of the huge building were lined with black rubber mats. There were wooden boxes at one end of each lane with a person standing in them to weigh them. Each of the four lanes then had four jumps leading to a sort of traffic light, then a row of duct taped hash marks going back about 50 feet. Behind that was a wall cushioned with foam. The lanes were fenced in with what looked like garden lattice, approximately three feet high, with feet made of PVC piping.

Rick watched groups of four dog handlers approach the nearer end of each lane. Each handler dragged the dog to a specific position aligned with the hatch marks. The dogs were fine with the manhandling and just stared at the box at the other end, trying to dig in with their claws, and they barked and barked and barked, or stared with predatory intensity at the wooden boxes at the other end of the lane. Some dogs yipped, some gave deep "WOOF"s and others screamed undulating bark howls. He hadn't thought it could get any louder, but as the teams arranged themselves and judges in striped referee shirts took their positions in between the lanes, the volume doubled, tripled, in a rising crescendo of sound. The judge raised his arms, like a conductor of an orchestra, and the noise coalesced into an undulating howl of anticipation. The hands dropped, the dogs began racing down the lanes. It looked like a relay, with another dog starting as the first finished, lapping each other at the start of the jump line.

After several races, Rick wasn't quite sure how it happened. Somehow, he found himself sitting in a chair just off the start line. Dogs and handlers lined up along the hash marks. A judge in a referee shirt stepped into the space between the lines. He held up a hand, locked eyes momentarily with a handler in each lane. The handlers were each crouched, holding onto a very intent dog. The racing lights started counting down. There was a momentary pause in the barking. And, then, the hounds of hell were unleashed. Dogs flashed past him as they raced down the lanes. Handlers screamed and beat the ground with dog toys. Tennis balls rolled everywhere. There was a pause. The judge held up a hand. Rick jumped as a person he didn't know was standing behind him barked at him to write the score. Everyone was looking at him, including the judge. Reading his confusion, the woman behind him with the neon pink hair pointed at blanks on the paper on the clipboard and told him to write "L" and "18.663."

It went on like that for three more times, then the dogs and handers traded out and others took their places. The person standing behind his chair was a bald guy with an awesome beard, then a young girl. In the blur of dogs and people, Rick gradually figured out the judge's signals and where the timer screen was. It turned out the people standing behind his chair were actually teammates of the competitors in his lane. They usually wore matching shirts, often something with pawprints and team names, pictures of the dogs, or some innuendo about balls.

The pattern of the racing changed. Instead of four dogs and handlers, there was just one dog and handler in each lane. There often wasn't anyone to tell him what to write, but he had the hang of it, now. It was kind of fun, watching everyone cheer for the dogs when they seemed uncertain. It was out of context and unexpected, so he didn't recognize the cattle dog in his lane until the dog came running down the lane, spit out the tennis ball and jumped in his lap.

"CYRUS!" It was Sylvia in the runback, screaming the dog's name and wiggling a fuzzy tug toy enticingly. He heard Donna chuckling behind him.

"I guess he recognizes you," she said.

Cyrus abruptly abandoned him and headed back to Sylvia. A tall, lanky, man tapped his shoulder, "Let me relieve you," he said.

"Guess I am a bit of a distraction," said Rick, and was released from his line judging duty.

He watched from the sidelines as Cyrus completed his runs, and then followed the two women in their "Ballistics" shirts as they headed out a side door, Donna keeping a steady stream of encouragement and advice to her teammate.

"Sorry about that," he interrupted. They both turned to look at him questioningly. "Distracting Cyrus like that, I mean," he clarified.

"Don't worry, it's not your fault he's a bit of a dingbat," said Sylvia, smiling ruefully down at her dog as Cyrus circled a bush, speculatively. "Besides, that's why we're here. He's working out some kinks."

"Guiness, my dog is pregnant," explained Donna, "and so we don't have enough dogs to field a team, but we still wanted to support the host group. They offered to let us switch our entry to singles when I talked to them about pulling from the entry."

"I thought he did quite well, actually," Donna said to her teammate. "He's starting fast, doing all the jumps, even holding the ball until he crosses the line. We just weren't expecting our friendly neighborhood police officer here." Both women looked at him questioningly.

The questioner is getting questioned, again, thought Rick. Aloud, he said, "Yeah, I just wanted to get an idea of what it was all about, this flyball."

"You think it's relevant to what happened?" asked Sylvia.

Rick demurred, trying not to affirm or deny.

"I'm sorry. I should know you can't tell us too many details of an ongoing investigation, but, yeah, investigating the flyball aspect is probably a good idea."

"And seeing if you can find out more about Jonathan's background?"

Damn, Donna was on the mark.

"Well," she continued, "Several members of his old team are here at the tournament."

Donna and Sylvia led him back through the building, winding though the various teams' crating areas and introduced him to some of the people. The women hung out with them for a few minutes. Donna explained how they were from Jonathan's new team, there running singles with the green dog to build his confidence. There were the obligatory comments about did you hear what happened? This led to a round of obligatory commiseration about how sad and awful it was, what happened to Jonathan.

"Anyway," Donna said, "This is Rick Austin. He is the police detective trying to figure out what happened. He wants to talk to you." She and Sylvia then left him to it.

"So much for your cover, huh?" laughed one of the clean-cut older men in the group. It then clicked into place for Rick. The man had a policeman's way of standing and moving. So did several of them. Jonathan's old team was mostly retired police and military. They were very cooperative. Under the cover of the constant barking they went into detail about their former teammate and what caused the break. But, despite their cooperation, he learned nothing new, just confirmed what Donna and her team had told him.

At the end of an exhausting day, he was left with ringing ears, and no answers. Plus, he lost the damn receipt for gas. Jonathan's old team did feed him, and they were easy to talk to. In the end, he didn't even bother reporting the overtime hours.

Chapter 18

Second Chances

"It's a second chance. A chance at a real life."

Sylvia was in the trees between the drainage ditch and James Fount's house, talking to the tent, again. At least it wasn't raining this time. Also, the tent was open. She could see William sitting inside, scratching her cattle dog's ears, thoughts churning behind the homeless man's eyes. She opened her mouth, drawing breath for more persuasion, then changed her mind. Sometimes, a person just needed time to think.

She was reminded of when she first brought Cyrus home and was trying to teach him tricks, Sylvia decided to work on "roll over." Luring him with the treat just let to him turning circles She tried luring him to the floor and just got a play bow. He just wasn't getting it. Cyrus was a bright puppy. He wanted to learn stuff and participated joyfully in the training sessions. Surely, if she could just get the dog to flip over once, and then gave him a jackpot of treats, he would realize the concept. So, she tried gently grabbing all his speckled legs and tipping him on his side. The dog frantically scrambled trying to get back to his feet. She kept trying, convinced if she could just get him to do it once, she could shower him in hot dog treats and they would break through this block. Cyrus panicked and wriggled out of her grasp. He ran off in the bedroom and hid. Even hot dogs wouldn't lure him back out.

Cyrus eventually learned many tricks. He could do hand stands and speak, sit, spin, pick up toys, say his prayers, weave around her legs, crawl on his belly, flip switches, the list went on and on. But he never, ever, learned to roll over and any attempt after that caused him to shut down and hide. Training Cyrus had taught her that it was that sometimes, you just needed to suggest and step back. Pushing too hard just led to resistance.

"I know I am pushing. I don't mean to."

Silence.

"It is something that has to be your decision. We'll support whatever you do."

More silence. Sylvia's voice was getting more and more hopeless.

"Everyone just wants you to have a chance."

This time her voice was pleading, nearly breaking.

"Even that policeman," asked William finally. He flicked his eyes up to meet Sylvia's gaze.

"He's the one that suggested this place!"

The man searched her face for the lie, but didn't find one. "What's the name of it again?"

"Here, look, I have the website on my phone." She quickly handed him her phone, and William scrolled through the site for the rehab center. Suddenly he stopped.

"California! How on Earth would I get there?" He started to toss the phone back at her in frustration, but checked himself and held it out for her to take back instead. She ignored the offered phone and said, "We'll help you! Please, it's a chance! Rick, the policeman, says he can arrange the trip. It will all be paid for. Please, please, think about it. You deserve more than this."

He pushed the dog away, crawled out of his tent and stood up. The branches behind her snapped. Cyrus leapt to his feet and barked uncertainly. William saw the young woman suddenly flinch at his height. She caught herself and stood her ground. He made a quelling motion with his hand. The man reached for her hand with conscious slowness and placed her phone in it. "Let me think about it," he said, his voice carefully soft.

"Okay," she said. She nodded to herself, and shifted her weight back, preparing to leave. In the process, she almost crashed into someone. It was the police officer who had stepped out of the woods behind her. There was a surprised squeak, but then the young woman recognized Rick. The policeman waved her on her way. Sylvia looked from him to William, who nodded reassuringly. There was a moment of resistance, but then she reflected that there wasn't much she could do, anyway. She turned and headed back through the trees, leaving them to it. Cyrus paused to bark a scolding bark at each of the men before trotting after her.

"That dog doesn't like us," said William.

"He's just letting us know not to mess with his person," Rick replied. There was a hint of warning in his tone.

"She didn't know you were there."

"Nope."

"Making sure the crazy homeless guy doesn't..."

"Trust but verify."

William paused. He could see the logic. Were the situation reversed, would he trust some derelict living in the woods? And the cop hadn't interfered or even made his presence known until the girl got spooked.

"If my daughter hadn't, well, I would hope there were people like you looking after her."

The cop nodded acknowledgement, his gaze steady. Then he spoke:

"Especially when she would go out in the woods to talk to murder suspects."

Now it was William's turn to flinch. There was a pause.

"But, what she said is true" continued Rick. "We can make this work. If you want to go to the rehab center."

"Trying to get rid of the riff raff? Send them off to California to be someone else's problem?"

"I don't shove my problems off onto other people," Rick replied, sharply. He took a breath and continued. "We're trying to give you a chance. And, away from your ex, away from your enablers and the dealer and the memories, you would have a much better chance."

William knew the truth of that. In his desperation to pry the monkey off his back he had gone to the library, faced the disapproving looks from the staff, and found the books. One of the librarians who worked there, a colorless woman with short, thin, straight bobbed hair had started out even more frostily polite than the rest. That was, until she picked up in his interest and apparently shared it. She had arranged interlibrary loans of the studies on addiction and recovery. He had read so much about mice that had been taught to snuff and snort and nibble on the bane of his existence.

He had later spied that colorless librarian so obsessed with the mechanics and tribulations of drug addiction at her home at 26 Cinder Lane. She was Brenda Burns, the wife of Buddy Burns, who was the neighbor across the street, who like to terrorize the neighborhood with his amped-up car horn and excessive gun collection. William wondered if she was doing market research for her husband and James Fount's little hobby. Everything turned back on itself, like a snake devouring its own tail. He did not go back to the library after that. The graphs and studies of knockout mice weren't going to help him, anyway. It has just been a distraction.

But, now here he stood, in front of his tent in the woods, with the policeman who seemed to be in one breath accusing him of murder and the next trying to help him get back on the straight and narrow. There was a little more back and forth, but as they continued, Rick confirmed for William that he would be able to go to the center, and try to get a life. By the time the officer left, William was feeling the first stirrings of hope. Hope can be quite cruel. You get used to things. Accept your fate as your due. But then hope sneaks up to make you do such very stupid things.

William probably would have been even more hopeful if he realized that Rick's intention as the policeman followed the little trail from the tent site to James Founts' house. The police officer ducked under the crime scene tape and made his way through the back door. Through the mudroom he went, and down the hall, back to the master bedroom and the closet and the panic room. That room had defeated them for days. But, earlier today, he had been told they had gotten the paperwork to cut through the door. It had been ready and waiting for him. He had planned to go through the recordings on the security system command center they found in there with Jeff, his partner. But Jeff hadn't been around much, lately, and they kept sending him out with that young prettyboy officer. Then the text had come through on Rick's phone that Jeff was on probably permanent leave, due to some issues with his drug addled daughter that Rick was trying very hard not to learn too much about.

There wasn't anything he could do about the implosion of the career of a man he had worked with for 15 years, a man who had saved his life and who's life he had saved, over and over. Drugs did that. They destroyed lives. Sometimes, you got a second chance. But, sometimes, your kid stole your work computer and hawked it for a high. And, sometimes, you couldn't resist trying to save your kid, by covering it up, as you had done so many times before. And, sometimes, Ricky, your work partner of 15 years who had looked the other way so many times, reached his limit and refused to frame the garbage homeless guy who probably had done worse, to save your kid.

So, Jeff wasn't there when Rick went through the recordings in the dark house. Neither was the prettyboy new guy. Jeff didn't see the video of the constant arguments between the homeless guy and the homeowner/drug manufacturer. Jeff didn't see the fateful night where James Fount tripped in the kennel, and he certainly didn't see who swung the door shut, locking the man in with his demon dogs and then fled the sounds as the dogs tore him to shreds. Jeff, his police partner wasn't there, but William was. Rick saw him standing in the open doorway. But, of course, William already knew about the events in the recording.

"I should have remembered the cameras." William's words didn't come as a threat, just a hopeless acknowledgement of his own stupidity. There was a long moment of silence.

"He kept recordings." William came in and collapsed in the other chair, his face in his hands. He lifted his head and stared bleakly at the screen.

"Well, you might as well watch the rest of it," he said to the police officer.

Jonathan had also starred in the recordings. He often came with money and left with the packets of the crystals.

"James Fount was a meth dealer," Rick asked. William nodded.

"And manufacturer."

Another nod.

"And Jonathan and you were customers."

Cringing nod.

"There's more," William said, and gestured to the monitor.

Rick pushed play and they watched together as, after James' demise, William appeared periodically, tending the dogs. Then he went into the garage and there was a long stretch of the recording with the dogs getting hungry and desperate before William finally staggered out of the garage, obviously recovering from a binge, stumbled to the kennels. He opened the doors and jammed the locks, let the surviving dogs free. He was too anxious to get away from the freed dogs to notice that Bad Momma dog planted in her kennel, guarding her puppies. William didn't see the kennel door swing back shut, trapping her.

"Those dogs were used to you tending them."

"Yes. James was scared of them. He would pay me in...well, you know. After, umm, he was gone, I was trying to take care of them." William looked down at his hands and swallowed. "But I, umm, it was just there and I, I relapsed. When I came out of it, I just wanted to smash everything."

William paused to swallow again before continuing. His eyes, staring at the blank wall, glistened with unshed tears.

"Venom and Glock starved while I was too stoned to notice. I don't know how Fang managed to keep the rest of her puppies alive." Williams' eyes were bleak. The police officer watched the camera recordings showing William headed toward the garage lab with a sledge hammer.

He was quickly chased off from his purging mission by Jonathan and the neighbor across the street.

Rick pushed stop and just looked at the other man.

"Buddy Burns and Jonthan, they worked with James distributing the stuff. After he, um, died, they thought it was a bonanza. They could keep it running and kept the profits for themselves. The police didn't even know James was gone. They wanted to pay me off in stuff, but I refused. I hoped the dogs running loose would scare them off, but Jonathan still went over there to try to make more. I, um, guess the dogs found him. I found bits of him all over."

"Was this in the garage?"

"In the lab, yeah. There was blood everywhere."

Rick watched William swallow, hard.

"What happened to it?"

"The neighbor guy, the one who was in it with them made me clean it up."

Rick's heart dropped. The chair gave a loud screech as he spun it to face William. "Steve was in on it?" Rick's voice was harsh.

William stared at him, blinking in confusion. After an eternity, he shook his head and clarified:

"No! Buddy Burns, the neighbor guy across the street. He likes big guns. He tried threatening me, but I told him to ... um buzz off. So, he said he would just shoot the dogs and Jen and everyone."

"And you believed him?"

William nodded, "Yes. He sicced James's dogs on Steve's sheep once, when I refused to do something. And, he sent one of them over to harass the people at Steve's place, but Steve managed to shoot that dog before it hurt anyone."

"Steve didn't shoot that dog. Animal Control did."

"Oh, I just knew it was shot."

"Steve didn't know about any of this?" Rick clarified.

"No, no, it was those three. And me, I guess."

Another pause. The house was so quiet. Life was so stupid sometimes. People made such stupid, greedy decisions and used others and ruined their lives. The house was so dark and quiet. The only noise was a low buzzing.

"So, do you arrest me, or what?" William asked.

"What" responded the policeman. It wasn't inflected like a question but rather a statement.

"Are you going to arrest me, now? Can I get my stuff first and clean up my campsite?"

Rick looked at the man sitting there, who had lost so much, and who wasn't offering any excuses or resistance. He wasn't trying to cover up or blame it on someone else. Rick thought about Jeff, who had been so full of excuses and trying to blame anyone he could for his daughter's and his own actions.

"No. No arrest."

"But, the recording" William met the police officer's eyes, then looked down where Rick's finger was firmly pressing the delete key. That explained the background humming buzz he had been hearing. He looked back up at Rick.

"Or, what." Rick's voice was decisive. He continued, "We're going with that option. You go back to your campsite, get what you need. Monday morning, I drive you to the airport. You go to the California rehab center and you stay away from that crap."

Oh, that dangerous hope. It makes you do such stupid things.

Chapter 19

You Deserved Better

The two policeman stood over the body partially buried in the leaf litter of the trees at 27 Cinder Lane. It was former home of James Fount, and now it was what everyone in the town was beginning to think of as "The Murder House." This really, really sucks, thought Rick, to himself. Everything was just getting wrapped up in a tidy bundle. Steve Henley had been cleared of any hint of wrong doing in the murder of his neighbor. James Fount was universally agreed to be a waste of space who was eaten by his own dogs. He had abused, starved and whipped those dogs into murderous monsters and seemed to deserve his fate. The older, unsalvageable murderous monsters had been euthanized. The younger puppies were with rescues. Any records of the security system in the house that might have shown where he was pushed, rather than fell, into the cage were conveniently destroyed. For a moment, Rick had felt empowered to be the "good guy."

And William, who had been the suspect, had been all lined up ready to be going to a rehab center in California.

Rick had taken the PTO. He was going to escort William to that facility and make sure he walked through the door. Rick had spent the night going over potential last-minute obstacles that might come up and making sure everything was covered. Energy and hope had thrummed through him. He had actually caught himself whistling as he got ready this morning. Maybe it wasn't quite right that some favors were called in to move William to the top of the rehab center's waiting list. He realized that list was full of similar hopes and stories. This was his story, though. It was a chance at a life no longer dominated by the tragedy of his daughter's death and an opportunity to shake himself free of the addictions that stole his potential and left him living in the woods at the back of Steve's property like a racoon. He deserved that chance. Didn't everyone deserve a chance?

But this morning, instead of driving him to rehab, Rick was at work, after all. William and all his potential were flung like an abandoned fast-food wrapper in the space between James' house and the dog run, half his skull blown off by someone with far more firepower than any sane citizen should ever want.

"He didn't deserve this," Rick spoke aloud.

His partner looked up from scuffing around in the piled leaves for bullet casings. Unlikely that he would find any, as the body had pretty obviously been moved. The policeman was so young, with sharp features and earnest, dark eyes. The man was trim and fit, with a meticulously pressed uniform. His black hair was slightly too long, and a little too artfully tousled. When the young detective's young wife dropped him off at the station and kissed him goodbye, running her hands through that inky black hair, Rick had a moment of whimsey wondering if some of the color would come off on the young woman's hands.

"Does anyone?" the younger man asked, as he flipped that ridiculous boy band hair out of his eyes.

Rick looked at him in confusion.

"Does anyone deserve to be murdered? That doesn't seem like the right kind of thinking for someone in our line of business," the young officer pushed.

Oh, we're one of those, Rick thought. Do I really have to try to justify myself to this idealistic child? Haven't I earned the right to not be questioned by my years of experience? Rick quashed those thoughts and reminded himself that being an unquestionable authority on right and wrong was not a role he wanted. That was for over-armed idiots blasting away others' redemption. We want good police officers, who engage, and ask, and don't make snap judgments. He needed to be honest, not defensive.

"Some do," Rick said, finally. His new trainee partner, Javier was his name, stared at him, disapprovingly.

"Some people really deserve what happens to them. James Fount was a drug dealer, an animal abuser, and an all-around ass."

"He was a citizen who paid his taxes so that we would protect him. And, this," Javier gestured at the body on the ground in front of them, "is just some homeless dreg on society."

Rick was surprised at how badly he wanted to punch Javier.

"You don't know his story. You don't know what he went through. He was just trying to..."

"Hey guys,"

Both their heads whipped around to see the newly arrived CSI, standing there, watching them argue. They both quickly shuffled out of the way and wordlessly headed back to the car. There was the sound of car doors opening and squeaking of the seats as they got in. Rick reached for the ignition button, then hesitated. He didn't want to be someone who didn't listen, who squashed any questions. Taking the moment, he just breathed in an out until the roil of anger choked back down. Talk, Rick told himself. You are going to be working with this guy for years. Have a better relationship than with Jeff.

"No," Rick said to his partner. "No, I don't believe people deserve to be murdered or assaulted or wronged. But sometimes, you just see someone is on the verge of maybe getting it together and having a chance after some really shitty stuff happened, and then WHOOSH! It all gets taken away. It just seems to suck even more, then."

Rick cleared his throat, staring intently out the front window at the leaves of the overgrown trees shivering in the wind. Rick could sense Javier watching him. He was not going to think about the home security system recording.

"I'm sorry about your friend," Javier offered.

It took a few minutes for Rick to silently smash down the overblown denial, the defensive anger wanting to write off his new partner as a passive aggressive little twit. Javier was a person, a coworker, who deserved respect and to be heard, Rick told himself. This wasn't Jeff, who used his position of trust to try to get his kid out of trouble. Finally, he was able to respond honestly.

"He wasn't a friend, really. I was actually giving him a lot of crap because I thought he was trouble and was causing trouble. William was just someone who was getting a chance. I just wanted him to have that. He was working his way back to being one of those upstanding citizen taxpayers." Rick congratulated himself for resisting the urge to add air quotes around the last bit. Youth and idealism aren't bad things.

"Let's find who did this!" Javier punctuated his resolve with a decisive slap of his hands on his uniformed thighs.

Rick nodded in agreement and then his attention was caught by the across the street neighbor's curtains twitching. Sneaky little busybodies are always watching, he thought.

He was distracted by the sound of Javier's door opening and the seatbelt zipping back into the holder. Getting out of the car, Rick joined his partner who was staring at the dirt in the driveway. The looked at each other and back down at the ground. "Drag marks?" mouthed Javier. They were surprisingly clear. Almost deliberately so. A heavy item had been drug through the dirt beside the gravel, leaving a clear trail.

Wordlessly, the two policemen followed the drag marks back up the driveway to James Fount's house. The marks led around the of the side of the house. No care seemed to have been taken to avoid broken branches on the overgrown brush. They continued following the drag trail back to where the trail culminated in the exact place the body had been found. Meeting each other's gaze, Rick and Javier simultaneously turned on their heels and followed the path of the drag marks backwards, around the house, down the driveway, towards the street. Across the street, a matching set of drag marks headed through the front yard towards the back of that house. The two policemen stopped at the property line of 26 Cinder Lane, Buddy Burns' house.

"He really didn't even try to cover up the drag marks?" expressed Javier in disbelief.

"Doesn't look like it. Not in the least little bit. I think we have some questions for Mr. Nosy Neighbor," said Rick. Perhaps a little snarky thought entered his head about how, if a criminal is this stupid, they fell in the 'better keep your day job' category, but his kept that to himself. Though, to be honest, Rick would have been surprised if his even idealistic man-child of a partner weren't having a similar thought. Besides, often, seeming stupidity had a purpose.

"What are you doing?"

Javier looked at his partner in surprise, his foot about to cross the presumptive property line at the edge of the yard.

"Going to the door to ask them to talk to us? About the .." Javier flipped the hair out of his eyes and gestured towards the drag marks.

Grabbing his partner's arm, he pulled him back, away from the edge of the property. "This guy's an idiot. With high powered automatic rifles. We need to get paperwork, first," said Rick.

The younger man tried to shake him off. "He will destroy the evid..." Javier's gaze flicked to the front window.

Damn those twitching curtains, thought Rick. Of course, they weren't twitching, now. They hung, straight and impenetrable. That house was very, very still. Waiting. Rick pulled Javier around to face him, held both arms to immobilize him, stared him straight in the eyes and said:

"We will take pictures. We will get paperwork." Javier started shaking his head in frustration, but Rick plowed on. "We will approach this in a legally unchallengeable way. We aren't going to go in there and get shot by an idiot who can't think through covering up drag marks."

Rick could have spoken more quietly, but he didn't exactly shout. And that house was already oozing with awareness of what they were doing.

Javier looked longingly at the door, but the resolve drained out of him. He turned and followed Rick back to their car. He got in and sat in the passenger seat, looking glum, but perked up considerably when Rick hailed the CSI guys and started pointing at the drag marks.

Once he had made them aware of it, Rick got back in the cruiser and told the younger man, "They are already here. They can properly document everything." Javier nodded. After a pause, Rick added, "And you have a wife who would miss you. Don't be stupid."

The younger man's struggle to overcome his own impulses and listen respectfully was clear on his face. Finally, Javier nodded more decisively.

"Thanks," he said.

Rick curtly returned the nod. Then they sat and watched the scene investigators methodically record the drag marks right to the edge of the property line. The curtains in the house across the street twitched continually, watching every move. Of course, when they returned the next day with the appropriate paperwork, the drag marks were gone. It was fortunate the police had rigged cameras to record from James Fount's house. They documented that, as well. The idiot in the house had time to think a thought, hire a lawyer, and turn himself in at the station for questioning, rather than panicking and shooting at people, especially very young officers with unkept black hair and pretty wives. Plus, there was now the additional option of charging for the well-documented destruction of evidence. Rick particularly appreciated the anticipation of the frustration the lawyer would feel at having to explain that bit to his client.

Chapter 20

Singing the Song of his People

J avier may have seemed brash and naïve at the scene, but in the interrogation room, he turned out to be quite skilled. Rick had himself removed from the case for reasons, but Javier showed him the videos of the interrogation anyway. It definitely gave Rick a new appreciation for the younger man's skill.

Mr. Curtain Twitcher was quite talkative. He was quick to start out saying something about an attempted robbery and right to defend himself. Javier nodded along, reassuring him about good citizen's rights to stand their ground and defend themselves and then lured him into self-implicating rants about homeless dregs on society. Javier had him tell the story of the attempted break in over and over. Each time, the details changed. The story got more and more elaborate. Sitting beside his client, the lawyer kept trying to reel him in, but the man was on a roll. Hopefully, the lawyer was paid well, because he had a hard job in front of him.

Mrs. Curtain Twitcher, the colorless wife, was a different story. She was led in, sat down and immediately dismissed the lawyer. There was no rationalization or abdication of blame. She sat, quiet, waiting in the room. All offers of coffee or water and any other attempt to warm her up and build a rapport to potentially loosen her tongue were politely declined. Javier came in, sat down and said, "Your husband tells me the victim was attempting to break into your house and he shot him in self-defense. Is that what happened?"

She had quietly sat at the table, head bowed, hands folded primly in front of her on the table. Slowly, her head raised, and she looked first at Javier, then directly at the camera recording the interview. For the first time, Rick noticed her clear grey eyes.

"No," she said, "That isn't what happened at all."

Javier blinked. He readjusted in his seat, repositioned his note pad, picked up his pen and said:

"Okay, well then, why don't you tell me what really happened?"

She did. Quietly, and with relentless dignity, she recounted a lurid tale. It involved white supremacist survivalists, a drug ring, and a lot of toxic masculinity. Her voice at first was so quiet that the microphone barely picked it up. Rick could see the faint tremors in her hands and the nervous swallowing. Her voice got stronger as she spoke. Javier nudged her a bit about why she stood by and did nothing to interfere with all this criminal activity, and that was when the descriptions of abuse and threats, the guns pointed at her head came out. There was the scratching sound of Javier's pen as he took notes on what could be potentially verified. Rick saw her eyes flick to make sure he noted the verifiable details. She wasn't stupid, Rick realized, and she wasn't weak.

She knew this was her chance to get out, and she was taking it.

When she got to the night in question, Brenda Burns' voice got quieter, again. The trembling was visible even in the video. It turned out that in addition to Mr. Curtain Twitcher and Colorless Wife, there was also a Stupid Teenage Son named Mason. Mason took after daddy in ideology. She didn't like talking about this, and spoke to the wall, rather than to her interviewer. But, still, she told. Mason was following in his father's footsteps, helping to raise money for political campaigns by brewing meth. Unknown to his parents, he began giving away samples of the merchandise to a hot girl in his class. The hot girl was the daughter of a local policeman. Rick flinched, when he heard that. With the death of Fount, and police investigators swarming the lab, Mason lost his supply. Hot girl was shopping around to get stuff from other sources. So, he snuck over to the house one night to make a little something to buy her attention. William surprised him and chased him off.

This happened several times, and this last time, Mason had succeeded in making a batch. He tried to leave with the goods and William tried to chase him down. Being a bright boy, he ran straight across the street to his parents' home. At the doorway, William stopped and pleaded with his parents to take the stuff away and not let him use it to destroy more lives. Mr. Curtain Twitcher just yelled at the homeless trash to shut up and go away. The wife grabbed her husband's arm, pleading with him that they needed to stop this, stop the drugs, stop destroying lives. Meanwhile, Mason found one of his father's bigger guns and shot William.

Twice.

Brenda described being frozen in shock. This felt more real than the extremist podcasts and side job of meth brewing. This was an actual person, that she had talked to. She even knew his name. She was told they would do the same thing to her if she opened her stupid mouth. They shoved her in the bathroom, put a chair under the doorknob, and then husband and son shouted and argued about every step of what they needed to do to get the body moved from the back door. They would need to bury it in a shallow grave, clean up the blood, hide the gun and the spent bullet casings.

Javier showed his interrogation skills by not interrupting to point out how that didn't match the evidence. He did not confront her about the drag marks or the different location of the body. He just listened and let her tell her tale. Because, when it came down to it, she was the only one in the room who actually knew what happened. He let her talk.

So, knowing her husband was not intellectually gifted, Brenda acted appropriately intimidated, and, after son and husband dozed off, she had crawled out the bathroom window. She found the gun in the guest room toilet tank in a baggie and replaced it in the prominent gun case. Mrs. Curtain Twitcher described digging the spent shot casings out of the burn barrel and positioning them by the back door. Brenda told the story of how she found the shallow grave, dug up William and carried him to the back door of her own house. Carefully, she disguised the grave where she had found him, and the marks dragging him to the back door. Then, she drug him slowly and heavily from the back door to the still actively investigated crime scene next door. She made a quick call to the tipline and then she waited until she was in police custody to open her not so stupid mouth.

"Wow," said Rick, rocking back in his chair.

Javier sat there, just grinning at him.

"Is she making it up? Is she trying to cover up something else?"

"What would she be covering up? Besides, we verified everything."

Rick eyed him dubiously.

"Well, not EVERYthing," Javier clarified, "but, enough. Enough to charge them and probably convict."

"Are you going to charge her?"

"With what?"

Rick looked at him. "I can think of a few things," he said.

"Yeah, but, I mean..."

"You're not charging her."

"Nope. Nada. Nothing."

"Wow," said Rick again. He didn't voice it, but he couldn't help thinking that Mrs. Colorless was quite the stealthy little thing. It seems that she could take care of herself and hold the line, when needed. Even if fate and stupidity insisted that William didn't make it out of this, he was kind of glad she did. It wasn't just because of her pretty grey eyes, either. He had seen many pretty on the outside awful on the inside types, and many pretty little victims. This lady was not a damsel in distress looking to be rescued. Brenda Burns was a warrior in her own right.

Chapter 21

Retirement Party

'So long, QUITTER! You're DEAD to us!' read the cake, in virulent purple lettering. It was a standard bakery sheet cake from ABC Bakery, yellow cake with chocolate buttercream frosting. Rick thought it oddly sweet that his soon to be ex coworkers would know his favorite flavor. There were the obligatory plastic flotsam decorations of little police badges and guns and even a black and white police cruiser. Apparently, Rick's coworkers couldn't quite hold to the gruff humor and had written 'We'll miss you' and "Good Luck!' on the accompanying card. The main office of the station was decorated in crepe paper and balloons. When he opened the drawers to his desk, those little paper pop up snakes had leapt out. One drawer had the singing fish rigged to go off.

Rick endured the obligatory razzing and backslapping. Sally, from dispatch, had some pretty good embarrassing stories and even a recording she played of a particularly bizarre and confusing call about an escaped ostrich that ended up in Walmart. Rick had screamed like a schoolgirl when they were shooing that thing down the aisle toward the door and it suddenly turned and ran straight back at them. Javier also gave an awkward speech about some close calls and how in the short time they had worked together he had learned so much from Rick. Then he handed the older man a gift bag with "congratulations!" printed on it in bright colors and several balloons tied to it. Nestled in amongst the crumpled tissue was a beer stein that they had made for him praising the glories of getting fat, drinking beer, fishing, and sleeping in.

Rick had seen a lot of these types of parties in his years working in the police force. Now it was his turn. He would be lying if he pretended not to get a little misty over all the stale officer retirement rituals. But, in the end it was done and he was free. All that was left was the final cleaning up and clearing out. Before he could complete his quiet back door escape, however, Javier cornered him and simply asked, "Why?"

Why? Because he didn't want to learn about people doing stupid and awful things anymore. Because he didn't want to feel responsible for another person walking into their home, their sanctuary, and seeing it had been ripped apart looking for evidence. He had been the one who had driven Brenda Burns home after her interrogation and watched her face witnessing how her home had been violated. And, then, of course, there was Brenda herself. Rick had removed himself from the case pretty quickly once he realized the growing connection to this woman who went through so much and then found a way to fight back.

She should have been charged, for many things. It wasn't like with William and the erased recordings. He had only gotten away with that because of the chaos of Jeff, his previous partner's, career meltdown. "Adjusting" the evidence to prevent William being charged and create an outcome more in tune with Rick's preferences was a violation of public trust. It was a step too far. Just because he did not get caught doesn't mean it was okay.

He suspected that it was Javier that made any charges for Brenda just evaporate. Rick did not know for sure, and he wasn't going to ask. If Javier did it, it was because he knew about Rick's growing interest in Brenda. Rick did not want to be the inspiration for causing the idealistic young police man with the unruly hair to go down the road of "adjusting" things.

"Why what?" Rick responded to Javier's question, as they stood illuminated by a floodlight outside the back door of the police station.

"Why are you quitting?"

"Because I want to get lazy, old, and fat. Policework isn't conducive to that." Rick lobbed the trash bag from the can by his desk into the dumpster and let the lid fall with a crash. Something must have been startled, because they heard a screech and skitter in the dark.

"Why now, before everything is played out? We're in the middle of investigating stuff. Why are you just bailing?" Javier was persistent in his questions. Rick knew he was a gifted and persistent interrogator.

Rick looked at this earnest young man and could not figure out how to articulate how once you cross moral boundaries, like erasing evidence, you can't really uncross that boundary. It becomes always an option, when things aren't playing out how you think they should. He didn't want to be that person.

"Is it that Burns woman?" Javier asked. "You already removed yourself from the case. Just hang back until it's done! I will handle it!"

Rick winced at that.

"You don't need to fall on your sword like this!" Javier continued.

The night bugs swirled around the bulb of the exterior light of the station's back parking lot. The was a cool night breeze. Whatever had been spooked a moment ago by the trash bin lid had found a new space to hide. Rick hoped it had found some safe space where it could have peace, where its longtime coworkers didn't do stupid stuff and destroy their careers. Hopefully, it could just do critter type stuff and enjoy peaceful nights, and not worry about meth labs and addicts, dead people and ethics.

"I'm done, Javier. I am just done. I can't explain it any better than that."

The other man just stared at him for a moment, then abruptly turned away and stormed back into the station, slamming the door behind him. Rick sighed and then walked back to his personal car, climbed in and drove away.

Chapter 22

Noodle

"That dog was the source of all the doggie drama with Fur Fleet?" Jenny's husband responded to her amazed question with a disbelieving head shake. There was a collective flinch at the crashing sound coming from the flyball lanes.

"Yup, that's Noodle," confirmed Donna.

Donna, Sylvia, Jenny, Jennifer, Jen, Dan, Luis and Steve had their camp chairs lined up in a row in front of the crates. This tournament, their crating area was right next to the lanes and they had an excellent view of the start line. Over a hundred dogs were barking, screaming, yipping, whining, and making all sorts of over-excited noises all throughout the building. Judges' whistles, buzzers, and handlers shouting encouragement added to the solid wall of noise that echoed off the concrete floor and cinder block walls of the building. Dan dozed in the papasan camp chair while Steve tracked stats. The rest were watching the flyball races in front of them.

Among the racers was a young blonde girl, maybe 10 or 11. Everything about her, from her hair to her facepaint, was in shades of purple and yellow. She held a wriggling, yodeling terrier mix that was also decked out in the team colors, even the white bits of the dog's fur were dyed. The other three handlers each released their dogs in turn.

"Noodle must be the anchor dog," observed Steve. Sure enough, the girl released her terrier mix after the third dog. Noodle joyfully sprinted past the returning third dog and started jumping the four jumps leading to the flyball box. The little dog took off too early, crashed the first jump, launched over the second and third jump in one go, and barely cleared the fourth, before hitting the box, grabbing the ball, dropping it, leaping the fourth and third jump together, crashing the second, and hopping over the wreckage of the first jump. The girl quickly caught and resent her dog back up the lane, yelling "get the ball, get it, get it!" The confused dog trotted back up the lane, hopped over the heaps of the first and second jump, spied the reloaded ball in the flyball box and hurtled the third and fourth jumps. All the handlers on the girl's team, along with many of the fascinated bystanders, chanted "hold it, hold it!" Noodle did hold it this time and somehow managed to get over the remains of the jumps and return to his handler. The little dog spat out his tiny tennis ball and launched himself at the fuzzy purple and yellow tug the girl held. He latched onto the end and was twirled a full circuit around her, like a swing carousel ride at an amusement park, before coming back to ground.

A whistle blew. People from the sidelines hopped the ring gating to reset the jumps. The dogs and handlers lined up, and, four more times, Noodle's team ran, with similar results. The audience of fellow flyballers winced at every jump crash and cheered every time Noodle brought his tiny tennis ball back to his handler. Steve volunteered to line judge so that he would have an excuse to watch.

"He's a dog with a 13-foot stride trying to jump jumps that are spaced 10 feet apart," was Steve's analysis.

"They need to teach him to adjust his stride," offered Luis.

"They tried. He is too excited at tournaments. He's going to stretch out. They said they are going to have to retire him. The dog is going to hurt himself."

"Did any of the litter work out?'

"Nah. Besides, the trend is borderwhippets now. Border-jacks are phasing out as too unreliable."

Sylvia couldn't help thinking how that was what Jonathan had destroyed his whole flyball team over. This little dog that couldn't complete a single successful heat was what lead teammates to be thrown out of breed clubs, sanctioned, banned from competing, and lawsuits. Jonathan would end up shunned and go to their little town. It also, in a way, lead to him getting killed. It just sucked. Of course, getting involved in his girlfriend's brother's drug running and "Dog 'O War" breeding scheme had probably contributed to his demise. It was all such stupid stuff to die over. Flyball should be about fun and friends.

"Hey, we'll be in the hole next. Go get your dog warmed up!" Donna's admonishment startled Sylvia out of her reverie. She got Cyrus out of his crate, leashed him up, grabbed the tug toy she had braided for him and followed her teammates out a side door to lead their dogs to some bushes and then play tug until they were up. Too quickly, Dan rushed off to get the box ready and Steve said "We're up!"

Sylvia froze for a moment. This was it, his first run as the official start dog on the official team. They had worked so hard for this! She didn't want to let the other dogs on the team down. Sylvia was unable to make herself lead Cyrus in through the door to do their race.

"Don't worry, Sylvia, you're ready for this!" Sylvia nodded uncertainly at Donna's reassurance. Cyrus looked up at his owner questioningly. He started scanning around for things to bark at. Jenny appeared at her other side and gave her a quick supportive side hug. The dogs knew the drill and were trying to drag their owners back through the door to the lanes, claws digging in the grass and barking. Sylvia's human teammates more or less shoved her through the doorway and then over to the lanes. Sylvia shook herself to life. She started scanning the hashmarks, looking for her spot, dragging Cyrus with her. He fought every inch, digging his claws into the matting and squealing and spinning in circles, trying to dislodge her grip on his harness.

"He's ready to go!" laughed Steve.

"You think so?" said Sylvia, nearly pulled off her feet by her excited dog. His claws scrabbled for traction on the rubber matting.

Sylvia found 48 feet and kneeled on the ground, pulling a frantically quivering Cyrus into position, bracing his back feet on her thighs so the dog could use her as a starting block. The judge, standing between the two lanes checked in, first with the other lane, and then with her. Sylvia nodded, tightly. The judge raised his arm, racing lights next to the lanes started cycling through red and yellow. Dan's voice, at the other end of the lane where he was manning flyball box, starting calling Cyrus' name.

The dog Sylvia was holding suddenly froze, in perfect position, razor-focused on the box. As soon as the second of the yellow lights illuminated, Sylvia released the cattle dog and he sprung forward.

".4 Start! Not too shabby for your first one," said Steve, from the side of the lane. Jenny was dragging Flicker into position in the lane in front of her, preparing to pass Cyrus in the relay. A whistle blew. Sylvia jumped in confusion, breaking her trance. Jenny was dragging her aussie back to the side of the lane.

"False start on the other side," said Steve. "Get him back and ready to go again." Sylvia climbed to her feet, watching her little cattle dog hit the box, grab the ball and turn and then Sylvia swung the tug, smacking it hard against the matting and started screaming her dog's name and sprinting away down the run back.

It took a moment to wrangle Cyrus back off the tug and get him lined up again. This time, her start was a half second late. Cyrus was confused. The other team false started, again.

"Should I start him closer? Our starts are getting later."

"Cyrus will figure it out. Be consistent. Don't change."

"But,"

"Be consistent." Both Steve and Donna were adamant.

So, Sylvia told herself to trust her teammates. She lined her wriggly little eel of a speckly cattle dog up at the 48-foot mark. For that first race, the start times were all over the place. Second race and third race, it was a little more consistent. For the fourth race, it was .002, .001, .004, .01. Everyone was grinning at her and giving her thumbs up.

She could feel her dog crouching down and digging in as she held him at the start line and the start lights went through their sequence. He was really figuring this out and getting into the race! She didn't even realize that she got a .0000 start until she saw it on the Brag Board as she was walking by. But, then, she started getting early false starts. After the runs for the day were completed, Donna invited them all to her hotel room to celebrate the .0000 start.

"I'm so sorry," Sylvia began, "I just can't seem to get it right. He keeps getting faster."

"Which is a GOOD THING," Donna pointed out, as she poured the margarita mix into glasses.

"Not when I keep getting false starts."

Donna just laughed and handed her a glass.

"Can you just wait longer to release him?" asked Jen.

"I'm already waiting until the second yellow light."

Steve was already shaking his head. "Try moving back your starting position three feet."

"You want me to start him at 51 feet?"

He nodded.

"Okay...Won't that make us slower?"

"We're already pushing our seed time. We'll get a penalty if we are too much faster," Donna explained. Pick-up teams were hard to guess a seed time for, but with Guiness waddling around looking like she was stuffed with bowling balls, they didn't have enough dogs for their own team. Sylvia was just grateful Dan and Donna were able to make it to the tournament and support her.

Sylvia tried apologizing again, but they weren't hearing it.

"Just move him back further, take the time to find the sweet spot to start at. We'll do a faster seed time next tournament."

"And, we'll work on Cyrus letting Flicker pass him. He still puffs up and tries to take up the entire lane."

Sylvia took their advice, moved the start back three feet and there were no more early starts. The start time kept creeping closer. Cyrus was just getting faster and faster as his confidence increased. Which was a GOOD THING, Sylvia reminded herself in her hotel room as she massaged her dog after the last race, working out all the kinks and helping him settle for the night. She needed to get some sleep before the long drive home. The dog groaned with the attention and Sylvia loved feeling the way the dog trustingly relaxed under her hands. He should trust her. It wasn't like she would ever hurt him. Even if the dog had celebrated his performance in the flyball lanes by somehow getting the flyball bag off the shelf in the closet while she had been out to dinner with Donna, Steve, Jen, Jenny, and Dan, and methodically trashed everything in it. He had also chewed holes in every pocket of every garment she owned. It was probably payback for her obsessing over Guiness and the pedigree of the sire on the breeder's website. She was due to whelp in a month.

"You should look forward to having a little brother or sister to chew on," she had told Cyrus as she set the room back in order. Fortunately, Sylvia found the car key under the hotel bed.

"Good thing you didn't eat that. It would have hurt coming back out."

The dog just stretched, extending each toe, and that striped racoon tail, then sighed. Apparently, he was quite satisfied with having emptied every single treat bag and the hotel trash.

"I'm getting you a crate you can't get out of," she told him. Her cattle dog did not seem concerned.

Chapter 23

Dating

Despite his retirement, Javier would not let Rick quietly disappear. He insisted on keeping his former partner updated on every detail of the case.

"She is a cold one," Javier said, about Brenda one day. "She's the reason the whole thing broke open."

"Yup," said Rick, not looking at him. Instead, he focused on the patterns the creamer made in his coffee.

"Do you think she was the one who erased the tapes?"

Rick flinched. He could have said "What tapes?" He could have speculated with his former partner about what happened. Instead, he just sat there, in the booth at the diner. Finally, he raised his eyes from his coffee cup and met Javier's gaze.

"No," Rick said, "It wasn't her." Then he raised his coffee mug for a sip.

"Then who?" His partner persisted. Could he really not know? Rick was the one with access to the tapes. Rick was the one with an interest. Rick was the one who suddenly quit the force. Javier wasn't a stupid man. If he knew they were erased, he knew by whom. If Rick were inclined to lie, he would have questioned or expressed surprise and doubt that the recordings were erased. But, lying wasn't his thing.

Rick set his coffee cup carefully down on the table with a very soft clink. He looked at Javier. He hadn't worked with his young former partner for very long, but in that short time it became obvious that he was a good and dedicated cop, and a very good interrogator. They should be beyond cat and mouse games. Rick wondered if he would turn him in. He waited. Javier's hand was holding a tortilla chip. It paused there, in mid-air. Javier studied that chip. There was the background noise of clattering dishes and conversations from other diners. He could hear the waitress calling back an order to the cook. There was the sizzle of a griddle.

"Why?" as Javier.

Rick rubbed his stubbly hair, and then his face. It was a reasonable question.

"Why did you do it, Rick? I need to understand."

So, Rick took a deep breath, composed his thoughts, then told him about the story of William, and the tragic history with Jennifer. There was the drowned toddler, the witch hunt of a prosecution. He had been so full of self-righteous fire back then. The fallout from the mess of that case had tempered him with empathy. Hoping to share that lesson, Rick told Javier about William's despair and described the man's hopeless battle of addiction and guilt, and how William finally had a chance. Except for the recording from the security cameras.

"He killed them? Both of them?" Javier wanted confirmation.

"It looked like kind of a mix of accident and intent."

"And, now he's dead. Very neat."

Rick could agree that it was suspiciously convenient. He said, "No, just more people dead over stupid reasons."

"Was she involved?"

"Who?"

"Brenda, your sweetie."

Rick's eyes snapped back to the other man's judging gaze.

"What? No!" Rick slapped the table for emphasis, making the crockery jump.

"You sure?"

He closed his eyes, consciously focused on his breathing, trying to get his emotions under control. These were legitimate questions. They needed to be asked and answered. Once his breathing felt more normal, he replied.

"Yes, I am sure. And she isn't my sweetie."

"Uh Huh."

They continued with their rather quiet and awkward lunch and parted ways. Rick wondered if Javier might understand better now why Rick had needed to quit. He certainly understood his own reasons better. Deleting the videos had broken something in him. It was a step too far. He didn't hear anything further about it, so apparently, Javier was going to let it slide. He wasn't sure how he felt about that. Rick assumed that was the end of their association. He realized he would miss the idealistic young man, so full of life and hope.

It was with a little bit of surprised relief that he got the message from Javier a few days later inviting him meet for lunch to talk shop. Apparently, the videos were going to be overlooked. Javier admitted he had done some investigating to confirm for himself Brenda's lack of involvement. He also continued to razz Rick gently about Brenda. It felt more like the standard teasing happily married people give their single friends.

One day, Rick was over at Steve's house talking about plans to go on a fishing trip to Abiqui Lake. It was nice having time and freedom to do those types of things again. There was a knock at the door. It was Brenda. She seemed flustered when Steve invited her in to the living room and she saw him. They started out floundering about to try to come up with the expected meaningless pleasantries, but Brenda, standing there nervously twisting her hands, cut them both short.

"I just wanted to say I am so sorry about what Buddy did," she said, looking at Steve anxiously.

Rick and Steve exchanged a glance. Was she apologizing for the murder? The Horn Honking? The drugs? Honestly, there were just so many options of offense with Buddy Burns. And why apologize to Steve, specifically?

She picked up on the confusion and clarified, "I know he's done a lot, a LOT." There was a pause while everyone contemplated the many sins of Brenda's husband. "I mean when he would sneak over and mess with things around your house. It was petty and mean and I wish I could have stopped him."

"I don't need you to apologize to me..." Steve was waving it away, embarrassed for her.

Brenda wasn't having it. "I know, but I need to apologize. For me."

"Really, no, you don't..." Steve still tried to brush it off.

"Steve," said Rick, "let her apologize."

The woman nodded emphatically.

"But,"

"Do you accept her apology?" Rick asked.

"Yes, of course, but,"

"Thank you," said Brenda cutting Steve off. Taking a breath, she continued, "I know he damaged your roses. I ordered some replacement bushes and I will bring them by and plant them when they arrive." Then she turned to leave.

Steve started to protest, but Rick put a quelling hand on his friend's arm. The woman nodded to herself and quickly left back out the door before Steve could protest anymore. The door clicked shut behind her.

"She's trying to work through a lot. Let her work through it," Rick explained to Steve, who just shrugged in bafflement. Rick rushed after the woman.

"Hey," he said, huffing slightly, as he caught up to her in the driveway before she made it back across the street. He was a little at a loss on how to get her to turn back around. This wasn't a suspect he was apprehending. He needed to be social.

She turned to face him. "Um, I just wanted to let you know. Steve is an idiot, but he doesn't hold anything against you."

She nodded.

"I will explain so that he understands," Rick continued. "A lot of stuff happened. Do what you need to do to make your peace."

"Thank you. It, it just helps to separate what Buddy did from me. From what I did. So that it's things he did, not what we did."

Rick nodded in understanding.

"I get it. Don't worry. I will explain."

"Thank you." She turned away again.

"Brenda?" She turned back to him. Rick continued, "Buddy is an asshole. He did bad shit. You didn't."

A pause, then he continued, "Surviving isn't a crime." He squashed the thought that some of the things Brenda had done to survive were definitely a crime. Javier had taken care of that, somehow.

She nodded tightly, and turned away again.

When the rose bushes were delivered, Rick made sure to be there to facilitate Steve allowing Brenda to do her penance for her former husband's sins. He went to the garden store and showed up with a shovel and fertilizer and made himself helpful with the planting. Rick and Brenda discussed how Steve's mother had originally planted the roses. They debated which ones to put where. The roses didn't arrive all at once. There were several batches. Brenda had tried to get a good variety. Each time roses were delivered, Steve called Rick so that he could be there for the planting. There were more trips to the garden store to get trimmers and sprays, this time with Brenda and Rick going together. By the time it was done, they were a bit of an item.

During this time, Rick also continued his progressively less awkward lunches with Javier. During one of them, Javier was telling him about a case he was working on. There were a series of burglaries that local homeowners were very anxious to have resolved. They were getting closer and closer to an arrest. Rick tried to congratulate him on the successful outcome of his hard work, but the younger officer shook he head. He looked at the wall over Rick's shoulder and composed his thoughts. Rick waited. "I read all the files and news stories about that homeless guy and his wife. I talked to a lot of the people involved. Is that why you quit?"

"Most of that was years and years ago," Rick evaded.

"It bothered you, though, didn't it." Javier was persistent.

"Yes," Rick finally admitted.

"More and more as time went on?"

"Yes, but that isn't what made me realize it was time to retire."

Javier looked at him, disbelievingly.

"It was the home security recordings, Javier. The erased tapes. That was when I knew I needed to retire."

After a pause, Rick said "We already discussed this. Why are you bringing it up again?"

Javier looked away. The he spoke.

"It's just that, the more I work on cases, the more I begin to feel like putting someone in jail is a failure. Like we shouldn't be focused on ripping people out of the community and stashing them away. We should be working on keeping the community whole. Repairing. Is that stupid? Am I being too idealistic?"

"Probably. Probably that kind of thinking will cut your career shorter, make you less effecting at chasing down bad guys."

Rick paused, meeting Javier's eyes steadily.

"But, I don't think that means you should try to stop thinking that way," Rick continued. "I think you should try very hard to hold onto those kinds of thoughts."

Javier swallowed hard, nodded. and looked into his coffee cup. How many answers to moral and professional crises could be found in the patterns of creamer swirling in coffee?

If that whole horrible, tragic, mess that happened with William and Jennifer and their little girl somehow helped jar one policeman out of the "lock 'em up," our team vs their team mentality, well at least something good came out of it. If he ever had a chance, he was going to tell Jennifer that. Well, if she didn't slug him first. Jennifer was a woman of strong opinions. Kind of like his Brenda. Brenda was really finding her voice and not putting up with any bs from anyone. Rick realized he was smiling to himself like a dufus. Maybe being a dufus was a good thing to be.

Chapter 24

Rainbows and Puppies

"I can't believe we're finally going to get to practice!" Jenny stretched her arms and shook out her onyx ringlets, reveling in the early spring sunshine at Steve's place. Luis paused a moment to admire his young wife, until Dan teasingly nudged him to get back to loading the wagon with flyball equipment. They, Steve, Donna and Sylvia, were all in the barn, loading stuff on the wagon to be hauled out to the field for practice.

"Yeah," said Steve, "it's been a few weeks."

"Close to a MONTH!" corrected Donna.

"Really?" asked Steve, in disbelief. Sylvia, Dan, and Luis all nodded.

"Pups are gonna be crazy."

"Guiness is in early labor. Dan has been obsessed with logging into the puppycam."

"Do you know how many?" Sylvia asked.

"Marge took her in for an x-ray," Dan said, as he started swiping his phone. Finding the picture of the x-ray, he handed it off to be passed around.

"Guiness is at the breeder you got her from?" asked Jenny.

"Yes. Here's the cam. It's a really nice set up."

Everyone dutifully admired the video of Guiness, flopped on her side in a specially designed whelping room. She panted and stared at the wall.

"Poor Shamu," sympathized Jenny.

"How many?" asked Jen, again.

"Marge thinks seven or eight!"

"Wow, poor girlie." The team dogs started gathering around. There was a lot of doggy energy with no place to direct it safely, so Jen and Jennifer headed out to the field. Jenny grabbed the ball launcher and followed after them.

"Marge thinks it will be tonight?" asked Sylvia. Donna nodded uncertainly. They followed the tractor and trailer out to the field. When they arrived at the appropriate place, Sylvia yanked a folded wire crate off the trailer, set up with a well-practiced shake, and set her flyball bag on it. She reached for the next crate. A quick tug accidentally sent the whole stack of crates crashing off the trailer.

"Oooopsie!" it was said with more of a laugh than any actual concern. Those crates had been through worse.

"Her temp dropped to 96 degrees this morning and she looks really uncomfortable," said Donna, her voice full of suppressed excitement. They all gathered around Don's phone, looking at the screen. Guiness, on the video, was stretched out on her side, tail, legs and snout spread out as far from her oversized belly as possible, sound asleep. Everyone watched her even breathing for a moment, mesmerized.

The women started asking Dan for the link, but Donna suggest they all just come over to her house for a watch party when things got interesting. A puppy-watch text group was quickly set up, then they dispersed to continue setting up for practice.

"Poor things don't know what's coming when the girls start bringing home all those new puppies," said Steve.

The men took a moment to admire the pack of dogs out in the field, whirling around Jen and Jennifer, barking for someone to start tossing something for them to chase. The sunlight glistened off the tornado of black and white, specked, golden, and merle fur. Jenny was jogging over to them with the ball launcher in her hand. Some of the furnado broke off to swirl around her. The three women in the field started randomly walking to keep everything moving so that no canine squabbles broke out. Steve hopped on his little tractor, towed the now emptied trailer back to the barn and began reloading it with flyball equipment. Luis and Dan followed after. Sylvia and Jenny joined them. When they had loaded everything, he started towing the loaded trailer back out to the field. The other four followed along, catching whatever fell. Sylvia wondered how much gas they used, towing that little trailer back and forth each practice. It's worth it, she decided, as she helped Dan position the heavy flyball boxes.

"I wonder if the new people will show up," mused Donna.

"New people? Who? What kind of dog?" asked Jennifer. She was used to being the source of new recruits.

"Shelter dog? Guy and his girlfriend. Dog is named Bullet."

"Oh, they contacted you?" asked Steve. "I gave them your info. He's been talking about how Bullet has a lot of energy, and they want to find an outlet."

"Hope it has some drive."

"Oh," said Sylvia, as she looked back at the couple getting their dog out of the car in the driveway, "I think so."

Luis followed her gaze and froze.

"That's a freakin' Mal."

"Yup," said Steve, smirking.

"Wait, is that...?"

It was. Former Police Officer Rick Austin, looking awkward in civilian clothes, was walking through the gate and up the field toward them. He had something fluffy and white tucked under his arm. His other arm was around a chunky woman with rainbow-dyed pixie haircut. She was tightly holding the leash of what looked like a working-line Malinois. Donna shot Steve a glance, then hurried over to talk them through the doggie introduction process.

"Cyrus, LEAVE IT, that is NOT APPROPRIATE!" Syvia screamed. The cattle dog had broken away from the rest of the pack and shot like an arrow straight for the newcomers. Sylvia watched, transfixed in fear that her adventurous dog might actually suffer the consequences of his actions this time.

There is a concept in some science fiction where a spaceship "sling shots" around the gravity well of a planet to gain momentum back in the direction it came from (or travel back in time, or whatever.) Cyrus elected to perform a similar type of maneuver, whipping around the couple with the mal and heading back to his owner. The lady holding the Malinois managed to keep hold of the leash, much to everyone's collective relief.

Sylvia full-on tackled her dog as soon as he was within reach. She scooped him up and stuffed him in a crate. Then, she looked up to see most of the rest of the team dogs were also in their kennels. Steve's dogs, who actually had good host dog manners, were wagging hopefully from a respectful distance.

"Turd," she told Cyrus as she dropped a treat through the wires into the kennel for him, "I know you think you're a badass cattle monster, but that dog looks like it could eat you." Sylvia continued. She caught her breath and recovered her composure as the new couple approached. While it wasn't a stellar moment, she did admit to herself that Cyrus was making much better choices than a year ago, when she first brought him home from the shelter.

"Puppyturd," she said again, dropping more treats in his crate. The crate squeaked and thumped as Cyrus searched the treats out.

Steve had reached the couple by this time and greeted his friend with a quick handshake, which the friend used to pull him into a bro-appropriate side hug. While the rainbow-haired woman had the Malinois, the dog the man was carrying looked like a potential littermate to Steve's dog, Murphy. Must be an interesting household, with that doggie combo, thought Sylvia. The former policeman looked good, much more relaxed than when he was here in official capacity, a grin kept peeking out from the grizzle of a new beard on his face. They started sorting out for practice. Bullet, the mal, was pretty much as expected, hyper-focused and too anxious to work, but a nice, friendly dog who quickly fit in with the rest of the pack. Bullet and Shadow, Steve's puppy from the Bad Momma litter of baby wardogs next door, were soon quick friends. Apparently, the puppy had been young enough to be rehabilitated.

"Brenda is good with him," observed Donna, after they left. Everyone had been so distracted by Rick's arrival, no one had really noticed his girlfriend, Brenda Burns, at first. Her look was certainly different from when she had been Buddy Burns' colorless wife. Her hair was bright and spikey, her gaze direct. She spoke quietly but decisively. Brenda was done with hiding behind twitching curtains.

"She's the reason he left the police?" prodded Jen. She and the rest of the core team were gathered around the outdoor grill in Steve's back yard, preparing a barbeque. Well, everyone except Jennifer.

"No, no, not really," explained Steve. He squirted more lighter fluid at the coals, then quickly stepped back from the foomph of rising flame. Dan, who was standing next to him with the plate of prepared patties flinched and yipped. "He has been burnt out on it for a while. He just didn't really have anything else to do." Steve started arranging the burgers on the grill.

Everyone started exchanging pitying glances. Steve rushed to defend their impression of his friend. "No, I mean, policework kind of tainted everything. He needed something to pull him away."

"And dating the ex-wife of someone he helped convict was what he picked?" Jen looked a little judgy.

There was a moment while that shot was processed.

"I like her. She's direct. Knows what she is about," Donna said.

"Yeah, she seems nice, or honest, I mean."

"She's fun! Jumped right in. Sylvia even had her practice running Cyrus."

Sylvia nodded. "And, he didn't even give her any crap!" she confirmed.

"Well, there was that one little nip," said Jenny.

"Yeah, but she convinced him that was not approved."

Everyone chuckled.

"She came right up to Jenny and started quizzing her about hair dye and wigs."

Everyone looked startled by Luis' statement.

Jenny giggled, "Yeah, none of you guys ever say anything!"

Everyone flinched and looked at each other uncertainly.

"Sorry, um, we..." Jen couldn't figure out the words.

"Yeah, I know. You don't say anything about a black woman's hair. It's one of the rules. She just went right there and gushed all about it. I was like, Yes! Finally! Someone notices all the work I do."

"You always look so awesome, Jenny."

"Nah, sometimes I look ridiculous." This was delivered with a challenging grin.

Luis nodded in agreement. "She has this one wig I call the Glowing Green Tarantula. She wore it and Nobody said ANYTHING."

"Nothing! Not one word," confirmed Jenny. "I almost gave up." She put on a fake pout.

"Glowing Green Taran....?" Sylvia started to giggle.

"You know which one it is, right?" Luis asked. Sylvia nodded, her eyes glistening.

"There is also a purple one with orange..."

"And the spiky one."

"Hey, I LIKE that one!"

"Wait, it was wigs? You wear wigs?" Steve had turned away from the outdoor grill where he was flipping the burgers to join the conversation. Everyone turned to stare at Steve. They all collectively lost it, guffawing and snorting.

Once Jenny had recovered her breath and wiped the laughter tears from her face she confirmed, "Yes, Steve, I wear wigs. Or extensions. Or braids. Or whatever the hell I feel like that day."

Luis grinned at his wife where they sat together on the bench, and hugged her to his side, giving her a quick peck on the forehead. "You do you, babe, whatever way you want." He then stood up and went over to help Sylvia dig through the cooler to find beers for everyone. As Sylvia handed Steve a bottle, it was apparent that he was still processing this information.

"I thought you dyed it. Don't women do that, dye their hair?"

"Yes, but not EVERY SINGLE DAY. It would fall out."

"Plus, chemicals," commented Jen, as she accepted a beer from Luis.

"I do dye it sometimes. But I like being able to change it up all the time."

"Brenda's hair was pretty colorful."

"She did a really good job dying it. She said it was for Pride Month."

"Ummm, isn't she Rick's girlfriend?"

"Yes," said Steve. He looked around at their faces. "She's just supportive." There were more dubious looks. "She's an Ally."

"Okay..."

After they had said their goodbyes to the flyball team earlier at practice, Rick took Brenda across the street to drop off the dogs, then they headed out to Cold Stone Creamery as he had promised. It was a hard decision between Birthday Cake and Birthday Cake Revised ice cream, so she went with something that was a sort of turquoise blue underneath all the sprinkles and toppings. Rick ordered the same one he always did. They took their wafflebowls of ice cream over to the table and Rick watched her dig in to the treat.

"Your tongue is turning blue," he teased.

"At least I don't mix peanut butter and chocolate like some sort of heathen!" she responded, and stuck the blue tongue out at him.

He dug a spoonful out of his bowl and offered it to her, making sure there was a big dollop of peanut butter. She recoiled and shuddered, then threw her napkin at him. They settled in taking slow bites of their respective ice cream dishes.

"So," started Brenda, while looking intently at her spoon, "Remind me again why you insisted we stalk that Sylvia?"

"Not stalking, just keeping an eye on, like."

"Like a stalker. She seems fine to me. Why are you worried about her?"

Rick sighed. It was embarrassing to explain, and he could tell Brenda had her back up about it. She wasn't going to let it go, so he said, "I told you, she had a big scandal at that university she used to work at."

"If I recall, you said she was being a student victim volunteer in some brain study. They scanned her brain and decided to spread her medical information all over campus. So, why are we stalking her, again?"

"They found her results were abnormal."

"Her private, personal, medical results were judged to be abnormal by some psychology students who were still learning what normal was."

"They think she is a freakin' psychopath, Brenda! I agree that spreading it all over the school was wrong, but Yes! I am going to keep an eye on her. She is hanging around Steve and way too chill about talking to William all alone in the woods. I think she knew before anyone else ... Can you just leave it? Please. I gotta do this. What if she decides to turn on them?"

"Rick, be real. Those students don't know anything – that's why they are students. Her brain scan showed something. Fine. She seems to me to be a perfectly normal person living a normal life."

Rick was just shaking his head.

"Rick," Brenda said, "Rick, seriously, look at me." She waited until his brown eyes met her silvery grey ones. Brenda continued," You know what I did. You aren't insisting on watching over me."

"That is different! You were a victim!" Rick protested.

"Don't turn into Steve. You know I should be in jail. Sylvia is a victim. She had a hard upbringing. But she is making a life, and acting normal. She has a freaking pet dog. Psychopaths don't have pets. They don't have real friends. They are glib and shallow."

Brenda gave him a moment to reflect how unglib, unshallow Sylvia was. She would obviously do anything for her friends. There was some stuff, like how unafraid she had been that night she had confronted William in the woods. Maybe he shouldn't have let his former partner's suspicious dig in so deep.

Reading the drop in his shoulders and faint nod, Brenda conceded, "We can go to flyball. It's fun. I like them. It will be good for Bullet and maybe Malcolm. Absolutely no stalking, though."

Brenda and Rick did keep coming to practices. Bullet turned out to be quite adept. Snowy, the fluffy white thing, earned the nickname "Satan" and was awkwardly banned by Steve. The little thing wanted to kill Cyrus. It was endangering all the progress he had made and, at some point, Cyrus was going to take him up on it. So, the tiny white fluffball of attitude was banned for his own safety. Rick laughed it off and instead of the fuzzy little terror, they started bringing Brenda' nephew. Malcolm was a teenager, with long, Fusca hair and eyeliner. But, he and Fiest, one of Jen's little Jack Russells, bonded and quickly became indispensable. Malcolm also was quick to boxload, fetch tennis balls, carry stuff and do whatever it was that needed.

"It's nice having a kid around. All that energy," said Donna said to Rick and Sylvia. They were watching him tag team with Jenny and Luis to rev up Flicker, their black tri aussie. Flicker tended to be an overly polite frantic people pleaser, but Malcom had her swinging on the end of a tug and got some play "grrrrrs" from the sweet, gentle dog.

Rick said, "Buddy wouldn't let her talk to her family after Malcolm came out. He made her cut them off completely. Malcolm had wanted to get away from his family for a while so that he could figure himself out. Buddy took one look at him, standing on the porch with that hair, locked the door, and screamed at her for inviting 'that thing' to HIS house."

"Buddy and James were assholes," said Donna.

"Buddy still is. But he is in jail."

"Good thing the divorce is going through so quickly."

"Yup," said Rick.

"What happened to the son?" asked Sylvia.

Rick glanced at her. "Jail. Then rehab in California."

"The same one William was going to go to?"

Rick gave an abrupt nod.

"I am glad somebody got benefit from it."

There was a pause.

"Does the son talk to her?"

Rick shook his head.

"Well, hopefully, he is young enough to reform."

"Hopefully," allowed Rick. "He is pretty angry that she sold out his dad."

"And, she's pretty angry that her son sold out himself," snapped Brenda, inspiring a guilty start from the other three. Before anyone could come up with an apology, she stood next to Rick and wrapped her arm around him, leaning her rainbow-dyed head on his shoulder. "I think, hope, that he may come around, now that he isn't around his father." She gave them all a determined smile and nod, grabbed one of Bullet's toys from the backpack Rick had slung over his shoulder, patted her boyfriend reassuringly on the shoulder to let him know she was letting him of the hook for gossiping, and returned to where the others were practicing with the dogs.

"Sorry, didn't mean to..." Sylvia started.

"She's okay. Trust me, she would let you know, if she had an issue," said Rick, waving off the apology.

Brenda's family life sounded tense and complicated to Sylvia, but people have to work through what they have to work through themselves. You can give them a chance. She remembered the curling game at the winter Olympics that was all over television lately. You can frantically smooth the ice in their path like the sweepers in the curling game, but they have to travel their life under their own momentum.

Just like the stone in that game, they often curl off in their own direction.

Brenda's stone had curled off from the original path her life was taking, but it seemed a good arc to be traveling in. She smiled and laughed, and spoke her opinions. She was so colorful with her rainbow hair and bright clothes. Rick and her were affectionate and supportive of each other. There seemed hardly any resemblance to that timid, colorless woman who had hidden behind the curtains of 26 Cinder Lane.

Chapter 25

And Rainclouds

Jennifer was pissed. She skipped the puppy-birthing watch party that night. Donna tried to smooth it over by pointing out that Jennifer wasn't interested in getting a puppy from Guiness's litter, so it made sense she was less enthused. Plus, she was more rescue focused. "You know that isn't why," said Sylvia, as she pushed the blend button on the blender. Everyone else nodded in agreement. Jennifer could be prickly, but they missed their friend as they gathered on the couch in Donna's living room, snacking on various flavors of popcorn and sipping margaritas. Dan, picking up on the girls' night theme, had disappeared into his office, demonstrating the discretion that had helped build a strong, decades-long marriage. Porter lay spread across the women's laps, getting scritches and soaking up attention. There was some speculation on what Dan was watching back there on his computer. It was in jest because they all knew it was probably the same video of poor Guiness panting and circling, that the women had up on the living room tv.

"Wait, look! See how her tail is curling away?"

"Push Guiness, you can do it!"

"There it is!"

"Is it a puppy?"

The bubble of the sack appeared under the dog's tail and soon expanded until it popped and a messy, wet, limp-looking puppy appeared.

"Is it a boy? Is it mine?" Jenny asked. They watched on the video as the little limp puppy was scooped up, rubbed with towels until it wiggled and started to squeal its objection to being born. It was weighed, and the cord clamped. The puppy was a little male with a black face, big white collar and white socks going halfway up his legs.

"Handsome little guy."

"Love that dark face against his collar."

"Should call him Stealth."

"Are boys better, or girls?"

"Depends: do you want dumb but happy or smart but bitchy."

"So, kinda like people, then."

There was a round of obligatory cackling.

"Cyrus is a boy and he can be pretty bitchy and smart," Sylvia pointed out.

"He's an exception. And a cattlemonster. These are border collies. The girls run bitchy. The boys are usually happy go lucky."

Everyone decided to defer to Donna's wisdom on the matter.

"Oh, wait, is that another one?"

Guiness' tail was doing that weird curve again, and then she frantically twirled, plopped her butt down and licked. A similar bubble appeared.

This one was a classically marked red and white girl. It was followed by a blue merle girl, then a black and white classically marked boy. Two split-faced puppies arrived, one boy and one girl, with faces almost evenly split black and white. Another merle popped up. There was a long wait. Lots of popcorn disappeared. Finally, a tiny little black and white girl with an almost entirely white head and black ears finished out the litter. They spent way too long watching the puppies dry off, get their first nurse, and crawl blindly around the whelping pen. By the end of the night, the two mirror-twin split faces were dubbed Hansel and Gretel, and it was pretty much a given that they were going to Jenny and Sylvia.

The problem of Jennifer was a little more complex, though.

The rest of the team had tried to give her space, overlook her absence at practice, gave her time to process things. The lack of communication, instead of diffusing the situation, had just caused it to fester. Now, as Jennifer, Jenny and Sylvia were in the back aisle of the pet store, trying to work on getting Cyrus to let Flicker pass him without puffing up and scaring her, Jennifer's hurt and rage filled the aisle, suffocating any attempt at conversation. Jenny, after a couple of beers, had once described Jennifer as not an empath, but an outpath. She projected her feelings out into the world. Sylvia thought that summed it up rather well.

While she understood Jennifer's hurt, Sylvia missed her friend. She wanted to share with Jennifer the trips out to Marge's place to visit Guiness and the puppies. Sylvia would love to have Jennifer with her as she trolled through pet stores and Amazon looking for the perfect toys and supplies. There was just so much going on. But Jennifer was shut down and angry.

The dogs picked up on the mood. Flicker, usually a happy little wiggle butt of an aussie, was weird and timid. Cyrus, who had made so much progress on his reactivity, was barking and hyperalert. The breaking point happened when they were all in the back aisle of the store. Sylvia was standing next to Jennifer, holding Cyrus, while Jenny was trotting her dog back and forth by them to desensitize the dogs to passing each other. Jenny was mindlessly chattering, trying to break the tension. She kept mentioning Malcolm, Brenda's nephew, and how much he loved Flicker, and how much Flicker loved him, how they hit it off immediately, how much fun it was watching him work with her dog, etc.

Sylvia could see Jennifer twitch every time Jenny said Malcolm's name. Sylvia desperately tried to silently signal her friend to shut up about Malcolm, but the message wasn't getting through. Jenny was distracted by how ditzy her dog was behaving. Flicker veered over and jumped on Jennifer, frantically wiggling and doing the appeasement grin some aussies do. Cyrus snapped at Flicker and the poor aussie did a duck and twist out of her collar and bolted. Jenny and Sylvia froze, staring at each other.

"Why are you standing there? Go get her before we get banned from the store!" snapped Jennifer. It startled them out of it. Sylvia handed Jennifer Cyrus' leash and took off after Jenny to catch the other dog.

Sylvia followed Jenny down the cat food aisle, and they cornered Flicker by the kitty litter.

Sylvia saw her friend get the collar on her dog and Jenny's head turned toward the front entrance door. She started leading the dog that direction, and Sylvia caught up with her.

"I'm so sorry. This wasn't a good idea," Sylvia said.

Jenny stopped. Her incongruently bright wig contrasted with her dejected expression. "She's just so angry."

Sylvia nodded.

"Why can't she let it go?" Jenny caught herself, "no, that isn't fair. I get it."

"Yeah. Brenda was directly involved in her husband's death."

"EX-husband." Both Jenny and Sylvia jumped and whipped their heads around to look at Jennifer. "He was my ex. We were over."

There was a pause. Cyrus gently tugged at his leash until Jennifer let him return to his owner.

"But, he was a human being. He was starting over. We were absolutely done. But, he was starting to have a life. He could, finally, be okay." Jennifer swiped at the tears running down her face. "I wouldn't have to worry or feel guilty anymore. It would finally be over!"

There was a pause. Jenny started to draw breath to speak, probably to say something about how it wasn't her fault, but Sylvia nudged her and shook her head. The other two were quiet, letting Jennifer work through what she needed to say.

"He was going to be okay. And then that. Some stupid, stupid man shot him for some stupid, stupid reason. And that stupid, vicious man's stupid vicious son is going to the rehab place instead. That stupid, vicious man's WIFE is suddenly at our flyball practice. I don't want to think about her. I don't want to think about him. I don't want to! But Steve just drags them in and shoves them in my face!"

Jenny shoved Flicker's leash at Sylvia and went over to Jennifer and put her arms around her. Jennifer broke down, sobbing.

"And you all just carry on, like this is normal, like this is okay, like it doesn't matter!"

"It matters, Jennifer," said Sylvia, finally. "It matters. William matters. It so, so, so, so sucks what happened to him."

"What that woman's family did to him! And she just watched and said 'waaaaa I'm a victim, too!'"

Sylvia had a moment of discombobulation, trying to think of Brenda, with her vivid hair and straightforward manner, as any kind of victim. It's true. She had been. She had come through and come into her own, but she had been a victim.

"Am I just supposed to ignore that? Just pretend everything's hunky dory? Compliment her hair?" Jennifer looked at her accusingly.

"No," said Sylvia, after a moment. "No, I absolutely am not asking that. And I understand the way it was just thrown at you that first time they came was so not fair."

"That was Steve," said Jenny, "none of the rest of us knew. We were as surprised as you."

"I'm not angry at Steve," said Jennifer. "I know he is an idiot."

"He does tend to have rose-colored glasses," Sylvia almost continued on to comment on what a contrast that was with his friend, Rick Austin, the former police officer. Fortunately, her brain kicked on and she realized that now was not the time.

"Brenda offered to stop coming." Sylvia flinched at Jenny's comment, not sure how Jennifer would react to the woman's name.

There was another long pause. Cyrus and Flicker were surprisingly quiet. Perhaps a nose went to sniff at a bag of cat food. Maybe a cat toy was nudged just enough to emit a hesitant jingle. Jennifer wiped her face and squared her shoulders.

"No. No. It's good for her dog, Bullet. It's good for Malcolm. I don't want to do that to her."

"Then, what's good for you? How do we resolve this?"

Jennifer took a moment to process Sylvia's question.

"I am going to take a break."

"No! That's not fair! You are more important to us than her! Screw Brenda!" Jenny burst out.

"I am going to take a break either way. I need to work through some stuff."

Sylvia met Jenny's devastated gaze.

"We don't want to lose you. We would miss you," Sylvia spoke gently. She tried really hard to keep the pleading out of her voice.

"No, I need this. I am going to take a break, but I will continue doing stuff like this," Jennifer gestured at the dogs. "I was talking with the store about doing more classes. It was hard when the weekends were taken up with flyball practice, and I don't have a dog to run, anymore,"

Jenny drew breath to protest, again. Jennifer cut her off "I will still continue to work with you and anyone else from the flyball team…"

"Except Brenda and Malcolm," clarified Sylvia.

"Except them. I don't want to hear their names. I know I am being irrational."

"It's okay to be irrational. Just don't cut us off."

"Okay."

"And, come back to practice when you are okay with it."

"Okay."

Sylvia sat in her car in front of the house, thinking over their meeting at the pet store. Finally, she picked up her phone and texted to Jennifer:

- Are you really going to be okay with this?
- Going to be. Not there, yet, but I will be okay. Jennifer sent back.
- You sure?
- I held my daughter after she took her last breath. This is nothing.
- We never wanted to compete with that one. I would like for you to have easy. I want you to have happy.
- I will. This sucks, but I will be okay with it. And, you guys give me a lot of happy.
- Okay. Random cute puppy pic incoming.

Sylvia found the latest picture she had snapped of Hansel and Gretel, held by Jenny, mirror image faces looking directly at the camera.

Jennifer hearted the pic.

It would have to do, for now.

Sylvia tucked her phone back in her purse, got out of the car, let Cyrus out, and went in her house.

She thought about the curling competition she had watched. The stones go whichever way they are going to go. Getting in the way, trying to force a change, just gets your feet knocked out from under you. Jennifer was a pretty unstoppable force. Her rage and hurt were absolutely understandable. Sylvia didn't want her friend to get lost in the martyr complex trap and just disappear, but she wasn't sure how to stop it. So, she would just try to keep reaching out until maybe Jennifer was willing to come back to that sunny field at Steve's house.

Chapter 26

Muddling Our Way Through

Steve stood in the flyball box, bracing his knees against it, using every ounce of weight on his six foot four, bear-like frame to hold fast.

Donna and Brenda stood with Malcolm, a few feet away.

"That is an awesome tug!" complimented Donna.

Malcolm was holding a long, fuzzy tug toy with three holy rollers braided into it. Mechanix gloves were on both of his hands, along with gardener's arm protection sleeves. There may have been some extra protection under his shirt, as it looked a little too poofy on his rather thin body.

"Isn't it? He made it! Sylvia helped him." Brenda said.

"Jennifer helped," clarified Sylvia.

Donna looked over at Sylvia in surprise. The other woman was arranging the gutter and PVC stride regulator poles in front of the box.

"Oh, really? How," and then Donna caught herself, when Sylvia's eyes flicked towards Brenda.

Brenda grimaced. "It's okay, I know she isn't a fan."

"Sorry,"

Malcolm broke the awkward pause by opening Bullet's crate and letting the Malinois explode out. The dog immediately latched onto the tug, ferociously shaking his head and nearly pulling the teenager over. The dog managed to drag him over to line up a few feet in front of the box.

"Hold him here, right in front of his hips," Sylvia said, explaining the flyball hold. Malcom straddled the dog, holding Bullet in place as instructed.

"Now, wait until he is focused on the box."

There was the click as Steve pulled back the activator and started to load a tennis ball in hole in front of the box. The dog spit out the toy and stared at the box.

"No," said Donna, "no ball yet. He needs to learn his swimmer's turn first."

Steve stood back up, tossed the tennis ball back in the bucket and braced for impact.

"Rrrrrreeeeeedy, Rrrrrrreeeaaady," chanted the teammates, to tease the dog. Bullet responded by crouching down, eyes fixed on the box. Even his tail was rigid with tension. Malcolm released him and Bullet ran the two strides to the box, hit it with all four feet, triggering the activator, then sprang off. White plastic gutters and PVC pipe flew everywhere. The teenager stood there waving the tug. Bullet looked around in confusion.

"RUN!" shouted everyone, and Malcolm fled with the same energy and enthusiasm as if it were a horde of zombies after him, instead of his aunt's dog. Bullet sprinted after him.

Practices continued over the ensuing weeks. Bullet and Malcolm learned an awesome swimmer's turn. Flicker and Cyrus slowly progressed on learning to pass in the relay without veering off. Sylvia and Jenny continued to meet with Jennifer at the pet store she worked at to work on desensitizing the dogs to each other. They gossiped about practices and dogs and gradually, Jennifer seemed to become desensitized to mentions of Brenda, Malcolm and Bullet.

"So, will you or Malcolm be running Flicker at the tournament?" Jennifer asked one day.

"Ummm, probably Malcolm." Jenny said warily. She drew breath to explain about how owner-obsessed Flicker was and how the little black tri aussie would just wiggle and run back to her mom if Jenny tried to run her. But, she didn't. And Jennifer didn't ask.

"Is he practicing this stuff on Saturdays when you guys meet?" was all Jennifer asked.

"Yeah..."

Another time as Sylvia was volunteering to help at one of the obedience classes Jennifer taught, she found herself speculating about nosework, and if it would be a good outlet for Cyrus and Bullet.

"Probably," Jennifer agreed. "It's good outlet for energetic high-drive dogs." Then she explained the process of how you start the dogs and promised to email some of the homework papers and materials from when she was teaching nosework for a local rescue.

And,, so the breadcrumb trail gradually formed. One Saturday, Steve looked up from loading jumps on the wagon.

"Is that Jennifer's car?"

Sylvia turned to look at the driveway and it was Jennifer's car pulling up behind Brenda's little green Kia. They watched her climb out. She waved and they waved back. Then she walked around and unloaded a dog from a crate in the back.

"Hiya, is this Frodo?" asked Steve when she got closer.

"Yep, some kind of hound mix, we think. Thanks for letting me bring him out. He needs a bit of socialization."

"No prob," said Steve. "Glad to get your email and see you back."

Sylvia and Donna shot Steve a death glare.

"Let me guess, Steve didn't say anything to you?" asked Jennifer.

"It's good to see you," Donna started to assure her.

"Just surprised?" said Jennifer. "Kind of blind-sided?"

Sylvia and Donna nodded.

"Yeah. Steve isn't always good at giving people a heads up." Jennifer smirked. Then she headed out to the field holding the leash of a baying hound mix. Sylvia watched her march straight up to Brenda and introduce herself,

"I guess she's okay?" Sylvia's voice was hesitant.

"I guess. It's her call. Steve did say she emailed that she might come out, but we weren't certain, so I didn't say anything."

It is her call, thought Sylvia. Later, when Sylvia checked in with her friend, Jennifer was talking about Frodo's circumstances and said "You know how it is with rescue. The dog gets to decide if they are healed. If they are, then you have to respect that. You can't hold them trapped in a trauma they have decided to leave behind. It's not fair."

Okay, thought Sylvia. I guess you are okay.

"Well, let's get this going!" said Donna, with an enthusiastic clap of her hands. Dogs were rounded up and stuffed in crates. Jumps were unloaded and arranged. The flyball boxes were positioned at the end of the jump lines.

But Rick couldn't leave it be. Sylvia, Steve, and Donna were crowded around helping Malcolm teach Bullet to bounce back and forth over a jump.

"Uh Oh," said Donna. Sylvia and Steve followed her gaze. Rick had gone over to Jennifer and was talking with her.

"I can feel the freeze from over here." Dan had joined the watchers.

"Why is he messing with her? It's not like Jennifer is subtle in her feelings."

"Because he's a blunderer, like most men," Brenda had joined them, also. She glanced around at Dan, Steve, and Luis apologetically. "He is insisting on apologizing to her. For William, for what happened with her daughter, for all of it."

"He's poking the tiger," observed Steve, watching as Rick kept speaking, while Jennifer stood with her arms crossed, her body stiff. The sun glinted off of Jennifer's blonde hair. Even the strands of hair seemed tense in the way they fluttered in the breeze. "I don't think she wants an apology."

"Why couldn't he just leave it be?" asked Sylvia. "She was just getting past it enough to come back to practice."

Brenda shook her head and said, "I'm sorry. I told him she needed space, not an apology. He said he still needed to apologize."

"For him," clarified Luis, "not for her."

Brenda nodded.

"Fuck him."

There was a pause after Donna's outburst. Steve cleared his throat, "C'mon, now, don't. I know Jennifer is uncomfortable with it, and so is Rick, but you can't let things just lurk."

There were some disbelieving snorts at this. Sylvia started to compose a comment about how odd this was from someone who had kept a dismembered foot lurk in his trash barrel for over a week because he didn't want to report it to the police. That would be unnecessarily derogatory, she decided, so she restrained herself. She still thought it, though. Sylvia thought it really loud inside her head. She told herself to think about something happy, like how cute Gretel was now, as the puppies had found their feet and were bumbling around and developing personalities.

"I know it's not going to fix everything and Jennifer isn't going to magically be all likey-likey now that he's apologized, but it does show respect. It gives respect. Respect can get you through a lot of things that even love can't."

Everyone paused, looking at Steve again. Sylvia thought that Steve was a nice guy, and hated that he had ever been through enough to have that understanding. Maybe she should just trust him.

Everyone made themselves busy with various training tasks. Eventually, there was a curt nod from Jennifer and Rick walked away to help Brenda straighten the line of jumps Cyrus had just wiped out. The relief he felt was obvious in his smile and relaxed shoulders. Jennifer still looked quite tense as walked over with the rescue hound dog to rejoin her friends. Practice commenced.

Chapter 27

Cyrus' Tournament

Sylvia flinched and tried to duck her head under the covers to escape Cyrus. He had spied her checking the time on her phone, yet again. When the dog couldn't get to her face, he thumped both front feet into her chest and started barking. Sylvia yelped and twisted to the side to try to protect herself.

"Okay, okay, I'm too excited to sleep, anyway," she conceded.

The cattle dog triumphantly leapt off the bed and she heard his feet thundering down the hall toward the back door.

"You're a good girl, Gretel. You don't go beating me up first thing in the morning." Sylvia took a moment to stoke the little black and white border collie puppy still curled in a neat little ball by her feet. The puppy ball uncurled and waddled over to wag and accept her accolades. In the background, Cyrus barked demandingly at the door.

"Don't learn from your big brother. Cyrus is naughty"

She scooped up the puppy and wandered down the hall to let both dogs outside.

Sylvia and Jenny had each taken home one of the two mirror-image split faced puppies from Guiness' litter. Jenny had the little male that she had named Hansel and Sylvia the female, called Gretel. "We need to get some pics with your brother at the tournament, today," Sylvia told her puppy before sending her out to the back yard for morning duties. She watched as the puppy marched over to the designated corner of the yard and squatted, ignoring Cyrus as he raced around in circles, barking. Deciding that Gretel understood the assignment, Sylvia went back in to house to finish waking up. Theoretically, having gotten out of bed before the alarm, she should have plenty of time for a leisurely breakfast. In reality, lack of sleep from anticipating Cyrus' debut as start dog on the official team had her groggy and inclined to randomly space out, staring at the wall.

Because, it was finally happening! Cyrus was going to be start dog this tournament. Guiness had recovered her pre-puppy figure and they had been smoothing out the passing in practice. They were ready! It was going to happen. Cyrus' relentless barking in the backyard at 5:30 in the morning caught her attention out of her musing and she called the dogs in. Gretel immediately turned and trundled back in the door. Cyrus looked up at his name and then resumed barking at the fence. Sylvia walked out in her pajamas and slippers. She grabbed his collar to bring him in. As she led him back to the house, his tail waving like a smug metronome, she told the dog "Better watch out. Perfect Puppy is going to set a new standard around here." The cattle dog seemed unconcerned.

Sylvia gave the dogs their breakfast, Cyrus dined in the kitchen and Gretel was served her breakfast in her playpen. "No time for tricks this morning, Sweetie. Gotta get the car loaded. Sorry, puppy." Gretel watched her owner as Sylvia moved back and forth, picking up bags and carrying them out to the car. The puppy ignored the bowl of kibble. Somewhere in the endless trips out to the car and muttering about the ridiculous amount of dog luggage, Sylvia remembered to push the button on the coffee maker and toss some Pop Tarts in the toaster. In passing, she would encourage Gretel to nibble on kibble, but the bowl of food in the puppy playpen remained untouched.

Having completed the loading of the car, Sylvia went back to her room, escorted by her cattle dog, and quickly dressed in some paw print leggings and a team flyball shirt. Under Cyrus' watchful eye, she French braided her hair, found the trail running athletic shoes that some puppy had stolen and hid under the tv stand, and then sat down to her coffee and pastry. As she sat at the kitchen table and sipped, she ran down the list of what was needed for the trip. She could hear little crunching noises finally coming from the puppy playpen. "Good girl, eat your brekkies," Sylvia told her puppy. Cyrus lay on the shoes by the door, watching her intently. He was not going to be left behind. After she finished her breakfast, she took Gretel out back for one last visit to the still dark back yard before the car trip. Sylvia paused a moment to look up in the sky to find Orion's belt and the Big Dipper. Cyrus watched, unmoving. He refused to leave his station on top of the shoes. Sylvia finally extracted the shoes from under the dog and pulled them on. The cattle dog and puppy wiggled and spun, chuffing excitedly. The older dog pushed past her to sprint to the car and hop in the back seat, ready to be buckled in. The little puppy tried to follow, but though she was fast, she just wasn't big enough to jump in the car yet and had to be lifted. Once everyone was arranged, Sylvia headed out to the venue to meet her teammates.

"Be good, please," she told her cattle dog as she met his mismatched eyes in the mirror.

By the time she pulled into the parking lot at the fairgrounds, the sky was beginning to lighten. She cruised the lot until she spied Steve's truck. She pulled into the nearest available space and quickly jumped out to help Steve wrangle the flyball box to the field. When they got back to the truck, Jenny, Luis, and Dan were leaning on the truck, admiring the sunrise. Rick and Brenda walked up and the guys took over unloading.

"Well, I guess we're superfluous," observed Brenda.

"Oh, there is Donna!" The women walked over to help Donna set up the pop-up sunshade. Everyone grabbed a leg and pulled until the shade structure unfolded. Soon, a rolling cart loaded with folded wire crates appeared and the women set them up. Sylvia went to her car to get Cyrus and Gretel. Brenda and Rick followed her to her car and grabbed bags out of her car.

"Thanks! Is Bullet excited?"

Wordlessly, Brenda looked up across the parking lot at a loudly barking car.

"I guess you could say that," quipped Rick. "We decided to give him a chance to calm down before we take him to the field."

The team dogs were all installed in the crates. Sunshade panels and chairs were set up. Donna fussed over getting the banner hung. Donna and Steve headed off towards the voices yelling "Captains' Meeting!"

Jen had appeared at some point with her two little Jack Russells, and Jennifer followed soon after, with a bag of breakfast burritos. She and Brenda took over rearranging the set up and distributing the food.

"Where's Sylvia?"

"Over staring obsessively at the lanes."

Jennifer grabbed a breakfast burrito and went to find her. Jenny followed her.

"Don't worry, you got this," Jennifer gave Sylvia a side hug.

"Nervous?' asked Jenny from the other side. Sylvia nodded. "That's okay. Nervous just adds a bit of spice," Jenny said, with a reassuring smile and nudge. Sylvia nodded.

"I just hope Cyrus does okay."

"Cyrus will be fine."

"Cyrus and you will be AWESOME."

"Or, he'll find a dead body part. Again."

There was a collective snickering cringe.

"It's just a game. It's just fun. Eat your burrito, play with your puppy. Have fun!"

Sylvia nodded again.

Donna and Steve reappeared. Cyrus, Guiness, Flicker and Fiend were going to run on the main team. They had found a pick-up team for Fiest and Porter to run as alternates on. Jennifer took Malcolm, Brenda and Rick off to meet the other team.

"Malcolm seemed a little shocked that he is going to be running Porter," chuckled Steve.

Donna responded, "He'll get over it. Besides, Porter is pretty plug and play. He doesn't care who's running him."

"Do you think Jennifer will be okay?" asked Sylvia.

"She's run Fiest before. They're pretty used to each other."

"But, with Brenda and Rick?" Luis looked uncertain.

"They are all grown-ups. I talked to Jennifer last night, because I wanted to find a pick-up so that Malcolm would get to run a dog. She said it's fine."

There is fine and there is fine, though Sylvia. It was Jennifer's decision, though. If she has decided it's okay, then it's okay.

"All right, as long as she is okay."

Soon enough, Sylvia found herself in the run back area, holding a quivering Cyrus, trying to read the hash marks to find 58 feet. Donna stood, holding Guiness. There was Jenny with Flicker, and Jen with Fiend. Steve was at the other end, box loading, and Luis was holding the wire ball catcher. Dan was discretely pointing to the 58-foot mark on the tape measure reeled out next to the lane. She could see Jennifer's blonde Karen cut watching from the sidelines, next to Brenda's rainbow pixie cut, and Rick's bristly head.

Sylvia knelt and pulled Cyrus into position, his back feet braced on her thighs, and the dog crouched down, staring at the ball Steve had loaded in the box. She nodded at the judge, who blew his whistle and cued the start. The world narrowed down to the colored racing lights counting down.

Cyrus was unmitigatedly awesome.

She flubbed some stuff. She forgot to catch him after the first run and so he turned around for another go. He and Guiness met going over the first jump at the same time, her coming back and him heading down the lane again. Flubs aside, he was everything a good little cattle dog should be: focused, consistent and unflappable. In between runs, Sylvia watched for the pick-up team's runs and made sure to show up in the sidelines to cheer Jennifer and Malcolm on. She and Jenny would bring their bookend puppies and hold them up like baby lion kings.

That night, after she got back home and was soaking in the tub and watching her legs turn colors from the layers of bruises, Sylvia realized what she was remembering from the tournament wasn't the wins or losses, or the times. She was remembering the way Jennifer and Malcolm looked on the sideline for those lion king puppies and grinned when they saw Hansel and Gretel. She was remembering how she had been sitting next to Donna in the grass at the awards ceremony after the last runs. Gretel and Hansel were wrestling over the crinkly bee toys that all the dogs had been given by the host club. The pick-up team that Fiest and Porter had been on won first place in their division, and Jennifer, Rick, Brenda and Malcolm did an improvised line dance celebration.

"It's nice to see her laughing again," said Donna.

Yeah, thought Sylvia. She had spent a lot of time with Jennifer. She had seen her be patient, calmly working with overexcited rescue dogs. Jennifer had been passionate in campaigning for William, and for the Bad Momma wolf dog. She had been dedicated. However, Sylvia realized that she had not seen a lot of playfulness in Jennifer. It was nice.

What wasn't nice was trying to get up the next morning. It was still dark. Cyrus was obnoxious and in the way. Gretel again refused to eat without being hand-fed each kibble. Sylvia's thighs were covered in layers upon layers of bruises from being used as a starting block. Somehow, though, she got it together, got everything packed up in the car and headed out on the road to the fairgrounds.

Even though she was running late, she had no choice about veering into the donut shop drive through. It had to happen. And, they had coffee!

"A dozen?"

"Two dozen, please."

"What kind?"

"Have mercy, I haven't had coffee, yet."

The drive through attendant handed two dozen boxes of random donuts through the window, and something that smelled caffeinated topped with whipped cream. There was also some sort of box o' coffee and several disposable cups.

"Bless you, my child."

The window attendant laughed and waved her off.

When Sylvia got to the venue and waddled up to their team's set up location, everyone set upon her offerings like piranha.

"Legs a little sore?" asked Steve with a wink. Sylvia barely restrained the urge to flip him off, and nodded.

"Well," said Donna, "I have some Advil in the first aid kit. Better get 'em stretched out. We're the second race of the day."

Soon enough, she was back to kneeling on the ground, being a human starting block for Cyrus the Magnificent. There was no pick-up team today, so Rick alternated with Steve on being the box loader and Donna had Jennifer and Malcolm handling Porter and Fiest as alternates for their own team. Jenny and Sylvia were walking Flicker and Cyrus out, off away from the tents and lanes. The dogs' panting had slowed to a more reasonable rate and the two women paused to stretch out their dogs. Sylvia noticed Jenny staring off at something.

"Is that Jonathan's?"

Sylvia followed the other woman's gaze to a woman with spikey hair walking several slick and lean border whippets.

"I dunno. Honestly, I never learned to tell them apart."

"I think it is."

Sylvia shrugged. Jenny, however, made it a point to line judge so she could peak at the dogs' names on the sheets. She was stage whispering about it to Sylvia as they sat in chairs at the team set up, while Sylvia was looking at a pizza menu, trying to decide on her vote for lunch.

"Venom, Stealth, and Raptor – those are Jonathan's dogs."

Donna looked up from where she was sorting through her purse, looking for her phone, in preparation to go on a lunch run.

"Hmmmm? Oh, yes, the team that bought his dogs is here. Frequent Flyers, I think, is the name."

Jenny looked at Donna, a bit non-plussed.

"Yep," confirmed Steve. "They're winning every race in division one."

"Yay for them?"

"I am glad they are working out well for that team. It was a little problematic finding a place for them. His girlfriend wanted to sell them to us, but, like, they weren't housebroken or anything. They just live in crates and do flyball. We're not that kind of team."

"Was it a good thing to sell them to 'that kind of team?"

Donna paused, absorbing Jennifer's rather pointed question.

Sylvia could see Rick and Brenda's eyes flicking back and forth. She felt an irrational urge to offer them popcorn.

"No," said Donna, finally, "I don't think it would be a good thing. Frequent Flyers isn't 'that kind of team' either. However, they are the kind of team to be willing to take on the dogs and rehabilitate them as much as possible."

Steve chimed in, "It was worth it to them, to have a fast, competitive team. They agreed, though, to work with the dogs, divide them up among their team and teach them how to be pets, as much as possible."

Jennifer looked around, picking up on the tension she had raised. She ducked her head, slightly, like an appeasement gesture. "I didn't mean, I'm sorry. I was just..."

"You see a lot of shit in rescue. I understand that, Jennifer. But we did the best we could by those dogs. They are loved and valued."

"And, they aren't dumped in a shelter somewhere to be picked up by someone who doesn't understand the energy or prey drive," continued Donna.

Jennifer nodded. "Thanks," she said.

After Donna and her husband had left on the food run and Jennifer had disappeared to find a restroom, Jen observed, "Everyone is so prickly today."

"Just tired," said Steve.

"Jennifer tends to run prickly," commented Luis.

"She's just tired," said Sylvia. She didn't mean tired from the tournament. From the way Luis and the others nodded, she thought they understood what she meant.

Hangry, tired, or temperamentally inclined towards prickliness, Sylvia looked up to find Dan, Donna and Jennifer walking back toward the set up a little later, carrying bags and boxes from the pizza place, and laughing together. They seemed to have worked it out. Everyone in the team seemed to perk up after lunch, and silliness started. The dismembered foot toy appeared in Flicker's crate.

"Who put that in there! My poor darling! Let me get that out of there for you." Jenny was giggling as she removed the toy.

"She is just so aghast at this uncouth thing that appeared," observed Jen.

Sylvia said, "She won't even look at it. Poor, delicate, refined Flicker. What a thing to do to you."

Dan and Steve, the probable perpetrators, were guffawing at the dog's reaction. Rick just rolled his eyes and smirked.

This, thought Sylvia, this is the flyball that I wish Jonathan could have seen. She sat in the papasan camping chair with Cyrus in her lap, her friends surrounding her, laughing and teasing each other. I wish he could have seen the fun kind, the goofiness, the 'who really cares if we win or lose as long as the race is close' kind. She told herself that she was being a bit pretentious for someone who was so nervous and tense about how Cyrus would perform yesterday morning.

Cyrus stretched out in her lap, legs extended, toes spread out vulnerable belly just right there, begging for a tickle. Sylvia restrained herself, but relished the trust and relaxation in her dog.

By the end of the day, Sylvia was absolutely exhausted, and most of the rest of the team had that bleary-eyed look. It was a good kind of exhausted, though. When she got home, got the dogs settled, and fell on her bed, she slept the sleep of a rest well earned. Cyrus and Gretel slept curled up next to her, their rest equally well earned, toes occasionally twitching as they dreamed of future tournaments, or maybe just of tennis balls being thrown in the warm summer sun.